The Horse who Came Home

The Horse who Came Home

OLIVIA TUFFIN

First published in the UK in 2023 by Nosy Crow Ltd
Wheat Wharf, 27a Shad Thames,
London, SE1 2XZ, UK

Nosy Crow Eireann Ltd
44 Orchard Grove, Kenmare,
Co Kerry, V93 FY22, Ireland

Nosy Crow and associated logos are trademarks and/or registered trademarks of Nosy Crow Ltd

Text copyright © Olivia Tuffin, 2023
Cover images copyright © SHUTTERSTOCK, 2023

The right of Olivia Tuffin to be identified as the author of this work has been asserted.

All rights reserved

ISBN: 978 1 83994 643 1

A CIP catalogue record for this book will be available from the British Library.

This book is sold subject to the condition that it shall not, by way of trade or otherwise, be lent, hired out or otherwise circulated in any form of binding or cover other than that in which it is published. No part of this publication may be reproduced, stored in a retrieval system, or transmitted in any form or by any means (electronic, mechanical, photocopying, recording or otherwise) without the prior written permission of Nosy Crow Ltd.

The publisher and copyright holders prohibit the use of either text or illustrations to develop any generative machine learning artificial intelligence (AI) models or related technologies.

Printed and bound in Great Britain by Clays Ltd, Elcograf S.p.A. following rigorous ethical sourcing standards.

Typeset by Tiger Media

Papers used by Nosy Crow are made from wood grown in sustainable forests.

3 5 7 9 10 8 6 4

www.nosycrow.com

For Lou and Katy

Prologue

Yet another lorry. Rough hands, rough words. The pony was loaded up a rickety wooden ramp and recoiled at the strange smell radiating from inside. Beneath the acrid stink of the dank and rotten straw that lined the floor, it smelled of danger – of something dark and unseen. It was a smell that instantly drove fear into the pony's heart.

She went in quietly, as she always did, resigned to whatever fate lay ahead. She had no fight left in her. There had once been smart lorries with leather head collars and fleece rugs. But that had been a long time ago, alongside a distant memory of a girl who had loved her.

The pony trembled as the lorry shuddered into gear, taking a little comfort from the equally frightened pony tied next to her. Through the crack in the metal slats, glimpses of blue sky and a wildflower-strewn hedgerow reminded the pony of sunny hacks and pony shows, experiences she would have enjoyed in a different world, a world far away from wherever she was heading now. Somehow it felt like her journey was over, that her story would cease wherever she was unloaded when they stopped. It felt different this time. This was the end.

Chapter One

Hannah placed her arms round the bay pony's neck as she slipped his bridle off, allowing her cheek to press against his soft mane. The little pony's coat was warm after his session in the outdoor arena and his biscuity smell was heaven. Hannah closed her eyes as the pony nestled into her. For a few seconds she allowed herself to believe he was her very own. Everything else slipped away as they stood in silence, their breathing mirroring each other's.

It was the way she used to stand with Wispa: her face pressed against the mare's warm neck, looking down at her perfect white socks. She shook her head. The memory was still too raw and painful.

"Wolfie," she whispered, stroking his mane. His arrival had started to heal her broken heart.

Suddenly the pony pricked up his ears and lifted his head, and the moment was lost.

"How's the morning gone?" asked her dad. The rolling burr of his voice, so soft here, could fill a stadium and silence an audience. Henry Boland, showjumping Olympic champion.

"Getting there," another voice answered, and involuntarily Hannah's lip curled at the flat, clipped tones of Ashley the yard groom. He was the son of Johno, who'd worked for Hannah's family since before she was even born. But now Johno was retiring and Ashley was taking over, and Hannah *hated* him.

"Hannah's just ridden that bay," Ashley continued. "It's going well."

"Your name is Wolfie," Hannah whispered fiercely, and the little pony gazed at her. "And you're not an *it*."

To Ashley the ponies weren't Lennie or Silver or Bertie or any of the other names that came and went through Hannah's family yard. They were "the bay" or "that grey" or even "the useless chestnut". They were never a mare or a gelding; they were all referred to as "it".

Hannah had never understood why her parents, who professed to love horses, let Ashley talk like that. She'd asked them about it once, and they'd told Hannah not to overthink things.

"Oh, great!" Hannah's dad sounded pleased. "You know we've almost certainly got a buyer for him. That young showjumper."

As the two men walked away discussing the potential sale, Hannah slumped against Wolfie's neck. She knew a girl had visited recently to try him out. He was a beautiful pony, and super talented too, and Hannah knew he would fetch her dad an excellent price.

The Bolands took in ponies to train and sell, but only the *very* best. Henry bought ponies from all over Europe, taking a chance on their breeding or potential. Heartwood Stables was in such demand that often all twenty of their stables were full, and they were always under pressure to sell as quickly as possible so that they could begin training their next potential star. Prospective buyers would gaze in awe at the immaculate courtyard, the smart hunter-green stable doors, the pale sand of the arena flanked by a neat box hedge, and, at the end of their tour, the post and rail paddocks where glossy ponies grazed on lush grass. The Boland yard was the height of luxury, and nothing was better than a Boland pony.

If Henry Boland had time, and was in a charming mood, visitors would even be treated to tea in the tack room. Sitting opposite the top-of-the-range washing machine and a beautiful old Rayburn, Henry would talk his visitors through the highlights of his long and glittering career, gesturing to the ribbons and medals that covered every centimetre of the wall.

Wolfie nudged Hannah softly. It was his polite way of asking for a treat, which she always gave him after a ride. Smiling, she rooted through the pockets of her jodhs and dug out a Polo. He snuffled it from her hand and crunched it up, his sweet pony breath hitting her face with a minty tang.

"Hannah!" a bright, cheery voice called out, and Hannah rolled her eyes. Millie. And she knew that tone; Millie was clearly after something. Hannah gave Wolfie a pat and checked he had enough hay before reluctantly opening the stable door to see her sister, arms folded, tapping one leather-booted foot. Millie was the polar opposite to Hannah, who'd inherited her dad's dark hair, hazel eyes and short stature. Millie was tall and willowy, with flaxen hair that she mostly wore in a high ponytail. Her bright-blue eyes were beady as she looked over the stable door.

"You forgot, didn't you?" Millie's tinkly voice had an edge to it now. "I told you I needed to finish off Wolfie's video. Tack him back up. The light's gorgeous at the moment."

Hannah glowered at her sister. She had been right. Millie was *always* after something.

"I just put him away," she said. "It's not fair to get him back out. He's been a really good boy and he deserves to chill out." She didn't add that the thought of being filmed made her stomach tie itself in a knot.

"It will only be for five minutes." Millie was insistent. "Just get back on him. You know I'd ride him myself if I was as short as you. Dad's got that buyer almost ready to pay the deposit. I want to film as much as we can, especially as he's a big sale." She looked Hannah up and down with a pained expression. "Could you change?"

Hannah glanced down. Her faded band T-shirt and her old navy jodhs looked just fine. Out of nowhere, Millie produced a base layer and jodhs in an alarmingly bright shade of pink. "Ponydazzle's newest shade," she said in a triumphant voice. "It's so nice, isn't it? You know I helped design it?"

"It's gross," Hannah groaned. "I'll look like a giant raspberry. And, yes, you've only mentioned it a million times."

"It will suit you," said Millie. "Come on, go and get changed. This is Ponydazzle's biggest campaign yet. And they've chosen us – well, me – to front it."

"So you can then get hundreds of girls to buy it." Hannah rolled her eyes. "It doesn't look that different to the last pink one."

"Hundreds of *thousands* of girls, thank you," Millie said, preening herself. "My subs are at their highest ever. And it's completely different if you actually look."

As if she wasn't aware she was doing it, Millie looked around the yard, her gaze falling on the newly acquired show jumps in the arena, the top-spec wash bay and the waffle rugs hanging on a bar beside each pony stable. Hannah followed her gaze too and sighed. She didn't exactly know how it worked, but she knew Millie was behind a lot of the upkeep of the yard. There was *always* something to pay for.

"Well then, if I do this," Hannah said, "can you look at Jenson's newest video for me? He's made one about skateboarding tricks and he'd like your opinion."

Millie burst out laughing and Hannah winced, thinking about the way Jenson had asked her so earnestly to show it to Millie. He'd never have had the courage to ask Millie himself.

"Really?" Millie said. "He's got, like, fourteen followers."

"Over fifty now," Hannah muttered, but she knew it was no use.

Millie flicked her ponytail over her shoulder. "No, and why would I be interested anyway?" She shook her head, tapping a foot impatiently. "Tell him to get a decent camera to start with."

Hannah knew it was no use. Millie never had time for anything or anyone, let alone one of Hannah's friends. It didn't matter that Hannah and Jenson had grown up together; he was insignificant to Millie.

"So then why should I do this?" said Hannah, but then her dad appeared.

"Come on, girls," Henry said. "Hannah, don't argue – you know the deal. It's only a quick shoot."

"I'll tack Wolfie up." Millie moved forward, and Hannah sighed, the argument lost.

Wriggling into the clothes in the tack room a couple of minutes later, she watched as Millie led the pony out. She'd really miss Wolfie when he was gone. Once again, she felt the familiar stab to her heart. It felt extra cruel this time so soon after Wispa.

Wolfie looked confused about going back into the arena, but like the polite and well-schooled pony he was he didn't put up a fuss. Hannah trotted and then cantered him, trying not to look at Freddie, who did Millie's filming, as his camera followed her every move. Her hands felt all wrong, and she was already sweaty in the new outfit. She kept her heels rammed down; she dreaded being criticised online for her position. But Wolfie took care of her, flying over the jumps beautifully.

"Smile, Han," Freddie reminded her gently. "It is an advert."

Hannah adjusted her position and tried to relax her features into a smile, though she felt sure it would look like she was gritting her teeth. She hated being in the spotlight.

Freddie gave her a thumbs up as she passed him. He was always kind and patient.

He was studying media at college but had ridden as a child, and Hannah had to admit he did an amazing job on Millie's videos. He would often record really random things, like a hoof being picked out or a head collar hanging on a hook, but then he'd set it to music, adjust the speed and the lighting, and create something gorgeous. Millie's films stood head and shoulders above the others. But Hannah just didn't see the point. She'd rather be with ponies in real life than make a show with them for the screen. But then Hannah and Millie had always been different.

Seven years ago, when Henry had jumped his last competitive classes at the London International Horse Show, the whole family had been invited to join him in the ring at the end. Mum walked Hannah and Millie out into the arena to stand by their dad and his top horse Mistral.

Millie had worn a pretty velvet dress, her long blonde hair in a plait, and had waved and smiled at the crowd. Hannah had worn dungarees and tried to bury her face in her mum's sleeve. But in the centre of the arena she had found herself next to Mistral, who was also retiring. She'd wrapped her arms round him and could still remember the way his soft muzzle had felt as he stood so gallantly and quietly despite the noise and atmosphere.

The following day at school, while Hannah was hanging around in the playground before register with her best friends Gaby and Jenson, a teacher she didn't have for classes had approached her and asked her to sign a programme from the London International Horse Show.

Hannah had just looked at her. "Shall I take it home for my dad?" she'd asked, but the teacher had only beamed at her.

"If it's OK, can you sign it?" she said. "My daughter is your age and saw you in the ring. I didn't realise we had showjumping royalty in the school; she was so excited when I told her!" And as Gaby and Jenson had stared, Hannah had scrawled awkwardly on the programme, lingering on Mistral's beautiful face on the front cover, feeling utterly odd and wishing she was with him instead.

Mistral was gone now. He'd died a couple of years ago peacefully out in his field. He'd gone to sleep and just never woken up. Johno had told her it was the nicest way he could have gone, patting her shoulder as she'd gulped down huge wracking sobs. The beautiful horse was buried up by the woods with a simple wooden cross marking his resting place. Johno had cried when he'd dug the hole with the JCB. He'd tried to hide it, but Hannah had seen the tears rolling down his weathered cheeks. She couldn't imagine Ashley ever crying over a horse. For a long time afterwards Hannah had joined Johno and her dad in taking flowers to Mistral's grave. But gradually Johno had found the walk too difficult, and once he'd stopped going Hannah's dad stopped too.

Chapter Two

Once they'd finally finished filming, Hannah gave Wolfie a hug and decided she had to get out of the yard for a bit. She grabbed her riding hat and bike then headed out of the gates and freewheeled down the hill into the village, already feeling lighter.

It was a beautiful early-summer evening. The heat had gone from the day, and the air was noticeably cooler. She turned right at the crossroads, cycling past the village pub where a few men and women in checked shirts and work boots were gathered outside, tanned and dusty, laughing and drinking in the sunshine. Harvest would be early this year, everyone said, because of the heat. Her dad's medals glinted through the pub's window as she whizzed past. Inside, its bathroom walls were decorated with his framed magazine covers. Hannah bent her head down to speed past and then turned up a drive to a stone cottage set back from the road. The village was more like a small town these days, but everyone still knew everyone else.

Heartwood, the big grey house set against the backdrop of the rising moors, home to generations of Bolands, watched over the village. It could look beautiful or bleak, depending on the time of year. Today, as Hannah glanced back, it looked beautiful, the greens and browns of the moor softening the edges of the imposing building.

"Hi, love," a voice called, as Hannah leaned her bike up against the fence. Vanessa Mountjoy, smiling as ever, appeared from the side of her cottage. "Gaby's in the stable."

"Thanks, Vanessa," Hannah said. "How's Diego's leg?"

"You can see for yourself." The older woman smiled as they rounded the corner and the most beautiful black horse trotted over to the fence, uttering a soft whicker. Even in the field and slightly dusty from a roll his class shone through.

Hannah reached up to stroke the enormous black gelding.

"Doesn't he look good?" Vanessa said. "The vet is coming back on Monday to assess him, but they're amazed by how much progress he's made since the accident. It's been a long six months, hasn't it?"

"You've been brilliant," said Hannah. "Diego's so lucky to have you."

"He's given me so much," said Vanessa. "It's the least I can do for the old boy. All those ribbons, all the sashes won at dressage. We had such fun together. The vet says he'll only be right for light hacking now, but that doesn't worry me. I've got my horse still. I'm so lucky."

Hannah continued fussing Diego, thinking about the awful day he'd slipped over in the field. He'd sustained a serious ligament injury, and Vanessa had put in so much work to get him better.

A tabby cat sauntered over on the fence and Vanessa gave it a stroke. "I asked your dad if I could bring him up to yours on Monday," she said. "The vet wants to see him on the lunge on a proper surface and, as you know, my field's a little on the bumpy side."

Hannah smiled. "That'll be nice."

"I expect Diego must look around your yard and think, *wow*," Vanessa said wistfully. "He's always looked a little out of place here, hasn't he? It's all a bit scruffy."

Hannah looked at the stables. The doors had been painted pink and white one summer by the girls, and a few hanging baskets added a splash of colour. Diego and Muffin both had their own hand-painted stable plaques, created by Vanessa, who was a brilliant artist. Hannah thought about the stables back at Heartwood. None of the horses had a stable plaque, not any more anyway. Mistral's had been placed upon his cross and, on the day Wispa had been taken away, Hannah had shoved hers to the back of the wardrobe. Now no pony stayed long enough to have its own.

"I think it's perfect," she said. "And Diego's happy." *And he has a home here forever, not like Wispa or Wolfie*, she wanted to add. She still found it hard to talk about Wispa. Her throat would start closing, tears threatening to fall.

Then she caught sight of her friend leading in

the grey pony Muffin. A few months back, just after Wispa had gone, Gaby had stopped coming up to the Boland yard to ride. Vanessa, a long term family friend of Gaby's, had offered her the chance to ride Muffin, and Gaby seemed to prefer hanging out at her yard. Hannah was too proud to tell her how much she missed their hacks.

With her long dark hair and olive skin, Gaby could make the tattered old waxed jacket she had thrown over a pair of shorts and T-shirt look like it was from the pages of a magazine.

"Gabs!" Hannah waved. "How are you?"

"I'll leave you girls to it," Vanessa said, heading back to her cottage.

"Hey, Han." Gaby tied Muffin up outside the stable and turned up two buckets next to the wall. She gestured for Hannah to sit next to her.

Hannah sat down, resting her head on the cool bricks. "Wolfie's going this week one hundred per cent. To that girl who came to try him," she said. "Millie's been talking about deposits."

Gaby put her hand on Hannah's shoulder. "You knew it would happen, though, didn't you?"

Hannah sighed. "I did. But four months – that's long for us. I took him all over the county, showjumping, and even to pony club. And they let me do it – Mum and Dad encouraged me. I really thought ... I thought he might be one I could keep."

"Like Wispa," Gaby said. "Even *I* thought Wispa would stay. But I guess if Wisp went, there's no reason they'd keep Wolfie." She smiled kindly at Hannah. "I'm sorry, I really am."

Hannah slumped. "I tried so hard not to get attached, but how could I not? I miss Wispa so much."

"She was lovely," Gaby said, smiling. "I miss our rides."

"She *was* lovely. Those perfect white socks and that squiggly blaze." Hannah smiled. "I just miss her being around."

She bit a thumbnail, the tears that had threatened earlier now starting to fall. "Dad *told* me Wispa would stay." Hannah wiped her eyes. "He promised me!"

"I know, Han," Gaby said. "I remember."

"Although it was sad when the other ponies were sold, I knew Wispa would always be there. And now she's gone, and Wolfie will be too."

For almost two years Hannah and Wispa had enjoyed adventure after adventure together. Wispa had been the pony she'd told all her secrets to, shared her worries, hopes and dreams with. She hadn't even minded when Wispa had featured in Millie's videos. Millie had let her read the nice comments about the sweet mare.

"Have you ever watched Millie's vlog about her?" Gaby asked, and Hannah shook her head, wincing as she remembered the way Millie had tried to get her to talk about Wispa's sale on camera.

"I can't," she replied. "All that fake stuff she was saying when she filmed it, trying to sound sad. She told everyone I'd outgrown her. But I hadn't, had I?"

Gaby shook her head. "You know you hadn't."

"Even at our last show together, someone told me that I'd have years left on her. Do you remember how I tried to slow her down in the jump-offs, but there was no stopping Wispa!"

Hannah smiled, the memory of the feisty little mare fresh in her mind. As time had gone on, she had tried to downplay Wispa's talent. She'd deliberately taken the long routes in the jumps-offs, held her bouncing canter back, but despite this she was getting noticed. With her flawless conformation and amazing pedigree, combined with a jump that stopped spectators in their tracks, Wispa was always going to be in demand.

"I still can't think about that day," Hannah said quietly. "I'm so glad you were with me."

Hannah had just returned from a happy hack over the moors with Gaby, rosy-cheeked and wrapped up against a biting wind, and Dad was waiting for them in the kitchen. "An offer too big to turn down," he said. Then Wispa was gone the very next day, qualifying for the Horse of the Year Show within weeks, thoroughly delighting both her new owners and Henry, whose reputation as a producer of quality ponies soared even higher.

The night before Wispa went, Hannah spent hours writing her new owners a letter. She wanted to be sure Wispa would find happiness at her new home so she told them everything she could. How the little mare liked to slurp tea out of a cup, that she would bow for a Polo, that she hated red buckets and would toss them out of her stable in mock fury. That her favourite itchy spot was just in front of her withers and how she was able to take off other ponies' fly masks. Dad had promised to deliver the letter along with Wispa.

The day Hannah had watched the horsebox leave with her beloved pony was the worst day of her life. She was sure she could see betrayal in the mare's eyes as she kissed her goodbye, and, in turn, Hannah had never felt so betrayed by her family. She'd vowed never to get attached again, but it was hard. Every pony that came in had something special. From sweet little Seraphina who could pass the heaviest of lorries but would dance about at fallen leaves, to Jack who was an expert at undoing coat zips, and Velvet who could shake hooves like a handshake. And when Wolfie had arrived, he was so like Wispa. They had clicked immediately. Wolfie had started to heal her broken heart.

"I guess it all comes down to business, doesn't it?" Gaby said. "Wolfie was always going to be an amazing Boland sale."

"I'm sure he'll have a good home," said Hannah glumly. "At least Dad always makes sure of that. I suppose if you're paying that much for a pony, you've definitely got a nice yard waiting."

Gaby looked at Hannah. "I'm sure," she said.

Hannah frowned. She didn't usually like to know too much about the new owners. Some would send a photo or update to Millie through one of her channels, but for Hannah snatches of information about a pony she had grown to love only rubbed salt into the wound. She just had to trust her dad when he shook hands on a new sale.

"Anyway, once the pony is sold, it's out of your control." Gaby paused and looked over to where Diego was grazing quietly in the little paddock. "It's why Vanessa never sold Diego. She wasn't able to guarantee his future. Before the accident, he might have gone on and won big for a few more years, but she couldn't be sure, so she kept him safe with her. She'll do the same with Muffin too."

Hannah felt the teeniest bubble of irritation rise up. "I know," she said, "but Vanessa doesn't run a business like my parents do. She just has Diego and Muffin. Gabs, you know I *hate* the ponies being sold, but I'm sure Dad does the right thing. He's super selective about where they go. His reputation depends on it. They only go to the best clients. And ponies *have* to be sold for people to carry on riding." She realised her voice was getting louder and stopped herself.

"I'm just saying –" Gaby shrugged – "you don't fully know where they end up."

"I know," Hannah said again, trying to stop the edge to her voice creeping in. "And I would have kept Wispa too if it was up to me."

Gaby shook her head and smiled. "I know," she said, briefly putting a hand over Hannah's. "I know it wasn't your choice."

Hannah nodded but pulled her hand away. "One day I'll have another Wispa," she said. When she found her own special pony, her "heart horse" as Vanessa called Diego, she promised herself she'd never let them go. She'd lost Wispa, but she'd never let it happen again.

Chapter Three

The tension drifted away as Hannah and Gaby walked to Gaby's dad's takeaway shop. He always did a roaring trade on warm summer evenings.

Hannah took a deep sniff of the air. "That smells *so* good."

Gaby laughed, and they were back to Hannah and Gaby again.

"Is that a hint?" she said with a wink. "Come on, I'm sure there's something I can find you."

Hannah didn't need to be asked twice. Mealtimes in the Boland household were usually pretty basic, and Henry either read *Horse & Hound* or chatted on his mobile during most of them.

A few minutes later, Gaby emerged from the shop carrying two takeaway boxes. The girls sat on the stone steps opposite, enjoying the warmth of the evening, and Hannah took a bite of delicious jewelled rice and vegetables.

"Got another, Gabs?" A curly-haired boy propped his skateboard against the wall and took a seat next to them.

"We can always rely on you to turn up when food is involved, Jenson!" said Hannah.

Jenson, Hannah and Gaby had met on the very first day of reception class, and even with school changes and very different lives, they had remained best friends. Jenson was wearing a faded yellow T-shirt that matched the blond tips of his hair. Gaby had dyed them for him, badly, but somehow he pulled it off.

Gaby rolled her eyes, but she was smiling too. "Give me five minutes." She hopped off the step and headed back inside.

"Thanks, Gabs." Jenson turned to Hannah. "What's up?"

"Not much. Wolfie's most likely going this week," said Hannah, taking a big bite of rice to stop herself from saying more.

"Oh, Han!" Jenson looked genuinely sorry. "He was the brown one, wasn't he? With a white blob on his head? He came at the same time as that sort of patchy one, didn't he?"

Hannah smiled at Jenson's totally unhorsey description. "Yeah."

"He's been there ages," he continued. "I thought he might be yours now."

Hannah shook her head. "So did I. Millie's making a video about his sale. Dad's talking about a deposit – that girl who came to try him."

"Sorry, Hannah," Jenson said, patting her arm. "That's rubbish." Then he looked a bit embarrassed. "Did you ask Millie yet about my videos? I got sixteen views on my last one."

Hannah thought about the way Millie had laughed when she'd asked. "I did, but she can't right now," she said. "She's super busy at the moment. She did say, though, to perhaps look at upgrading your camera at some point?" She hoped it sounded as though Millie was passing on helpful advice.

"OK! New camera. I know mine's a bit rubbish.

That's good to know," Jenson replied brightly. "Maybe she'll watch the next one then."

Gaby returned and placed a box of food in Jenson's hands as he thanked her.

"But, seriously, why do you need her opinion?" Hannah couldn't help herself. "Why does it matter so much? Just enjoy your sport. I don't understand why you want people to watch."

"I don't understand why people watch your sister open horse feed bags!" Jenson retorted. "But look at what she gets, all those cool things she gets sent. And I bet she gets paid loads for her sponsorship deals."

"Yeah, maybe. But all that time she spends making things look perfect, when she could just be out on a hack, happy."

Jenson stirred his rice with his wooden fork. "Didn't you say she helps out your mum and dad with the money, though?" he asked cautiously.

Hannah felt a pang of guilt in her chest. "Yeah. There's always something to pay for. Dad's been talking for ages about extending the outdoor arena, and even building a cross-country course. They've got big plans – as always!" Hannah laughed and looked down. She didn't want to tell Jenson and Gaby about the official-looking letters that had started arriving a few weeks ago with red type at the top of the envelope, or the expression that had washed across Dad's face when she had passed one of these letters to him at breakfast. "The business takes a lot of work, and the yard needs constant upkeep," she finished weakly.

"I bet," Jenson said. "All those horses."

They were all quiet for a moment.

"Me and Jenson were looking at day tickets for Writley Festival in a few weeks," Gaby said brightly. "Want to come?"

"I don't know," said Hannah. "What's it like?"

"It's meant to be amazing. Hasn't Millie been?" said Gaby. "We could ask her."

Hannah shrugged. "I don't think she ever has." She couldn't recall her sister ever going anywhere that wasn't connected to horses or even just hanging around with her friends from school. Not for years.

"Oh, well. Vanessa's niece said it's so cool. And Lulabella are headlining this year," Gaby said enthusiastically. "Are you in?"

Hannah had vaguely heard of the band. Their music wasn't really her taste, but the festival sounded like a perfect distraction. She smiled, grateful for her friends. "Sure. Count me in."

Hannah sat upright, rubbing sleep from her eyes as she blearily switched off her alarm clock and opened her curtains. A pink dawn was appearing on the horizon, soft mist enveloping the sloping fields that ran up towards the moors.

She pulled on her jodhs and boots and slipped out into the cool yard. One of her favourite things was to wander around saying hello to all the ponies before anyone else was out.

There were lots in. Billy, Tolly, Micky, Juniper, every single stable was filled. In fact, Henry currently had two more ponies than he actually had stables, so it was a good thing the weather was fine and they could stay out in the fields. Ponies were always being sold, but no sooner than they left, another would take its place, the next big superstar.

After greeting each and every pony, Hannah headed up the path to her dad's one remaining horse, the big grey Delilah. Delilah was long retired now after an injury at a show meant she could never be jumped again. Henry had been advised to have her put down because she was worth almost nothing in a monetary sense, but instead he had made sure she was pain free and then left her to quietly graze the fields surrounding Heartwood.

To Hannah's surprise her dad was up at the field. He was leaning over the fence, looking as if he was in deep conversation with Delilah, who was snuffling her soft muzzle against his hands. Her once sharply cut mane was long and shaggy now and her back was starting to dip with age. She was the kindest horse, a yard favourite.

Henry looked up with a start at the sound of Hannah's footsteps and smiled. "Couldn't sleep," he said. "The mornings get too light too early, don't they? Thought I'd have a chat with the old girl."

"She was popular on your stables tour last week." Hannah moved closer and patted the big mare. "Hello, girl." She laughed as Delilah nuzzled her hair. "There were a couple of women crying! They were taking selfies with her. They told me they'd had her poster on their walls growing up."

"She reminds them of the golden days." Dad smiled. "It was different back then, when showjumping was more popular than football. We'd wait for *Horse & Hound* every week to read the latest news, and they'd even play the shows on the telly. There were whole days of it when Olympia was on; we'd set the video recorder. And when we weren't watching that, we were out hacking for hours, hoof pick tied to our saddle,

Thermos in a rucksack. No one knew where we were."

"I think it sounds like heaven," Hannah said wistfully, and her dad laughed.

"Johno will have some tales," he said. "Trying to dry all the jute rugs out on the clothes line, not like all the fancy quick-dry fabrics we have now or the heated rug drier. He used to cook up bran mashes on the kitchen stove for my dad. One Christmas it snowed and he managed to fuse the whole house doing it, but he was determined the ponies would have a warm breakfast on such a chilly day. We had cheese sandwiches for lunch. My mother was furious." He chuckled. "But she forgave him quickly; it was Johno after all. We lit candles and played Monopoly. Best Christmas ever as I recall."

Hannah smiled, and there was a moment of comfortable silence as Delilah stood quietly between them. "I miss Johno," she said.

Her dad looked at her and nodded. "I do too."

Hannah knew he understood. Johno was still there, but also not, at the same time.

She took a breath. "Dad," she said, "do you ever worry about Ashley?" She felt the atmosphere was suddenly sharper. "His methods, the way..." She struggled to think how to word it. "I don't know, just the way he does things. He's not like Johno."

Henry shook his head and stood upright, slightly startling his old mare. "Ashley's family, Hannah," he said. "I promised Johno his son would always have a job here, and Ashley has never given me any reason to doubt him." Then he looked at his watch. "Can't stand here all morning, I need to start work early today. Lots to do."

Giving Delilah a pat, he strode off back down the field path, towards the yard and his office where he seemed to spend most of his days.

Hannah placed her arms round Delilah again, breathing in her comforting scent. She wondered if finalising Wolfie's sale was on Dad's to-do list. Four months felt like eternity. Enough time to really bond, to work out all his little ways and sweet habits. She started to head back down the path too, her boots wet in the dew, leaving a trail of footprints in the grass. The curtains were open in the small cottage next to the gates, but Hannah knew it wouldn't be Johno up and about. It was Ashley, who nodded briefly to her as he emerged from the front door. He never had any small talk or pleasantries, and Hannah was equally cold back.

"We'll give Wolfie a bath today," Ashley said, his

voice flat. He didn't look at Hannah when he talked. "Ready for tomorrow."

So Wolfie's sale had gone through. It felt like a stab to her heart as she thought about the moment she'd just shared with her dad. Why hadn't he told her then? She wondered if it had even crossed his mind.

"I wouldn't ride him today," Ashley continued. "Last thing we want is to risk any sort of injury, not with the sort of money that's being thrown around."

Hannah felt her tummy drop. She'd planned to have a hack on Wolfie, ride up to the trig point, canter up the moorland paths where the ground was still soft despite the drought, jump the little gorse bushes and just enjoy what would probably be her final few hours with her sweet bay pony, and now she couldn't even do that.

"Not even a hack?" she asked, but she knew it would be no use.

Ashley curled his lip. "Definitely not a hack, and especially not one of your hacks. You'd be up there for hours. Can't risk it."

Hannah didn't answer. Instead she gave Wolfie a hug. She'd make sure she was the one doing his bath today.

"Tell you what you need to do, though," said Ashley.

"That chestnut mare your sister's been riding. You need to get up on it today and see how it goes. Millie's not getting a tune out of it."

Hannah frowned. There was only one chestnut mare at the moment, a pony called Tolly. She'd been so wrapped up in Wolfie she hadn't really got to know Tolly yet. She was bigger than the ponies Hannah usually rode. But she knew Millie had been having some trouble with her over fences.

"*Tolly* –" she emphasised the mare's name, not that Ashley seemed to notice – "OK." At least it would provide her with a distraction from the heartbreak to come, and Tolly seemed sweet whenever Hannah had done anything with her on the ground. She was also curious. Sometimes it was simply that a horse responded better to a different rider, and however beautifully Millie rode, perhaps she and Tolly just hadn't clicked.

A short while later, and having completed her yard jobs, Hannah headed back into the house for breakfast and to change into her riding clothes. *At least I don't have to wear those awful pink jodhs*, she thought, wriggling into her favourite old navy pair. She wasn't quite sure where Millie was, but she was hoping to ride Tolly quietly in the top arena by herself, with as few people watching as possible. Millie saw everything as a photo or video opportunity, and Hannah just wanted to get to know the chestnut pony by herself. Cramming some toast into her mouth and heading for the door, she bumped straight into her dad, who was looking unusually smart.

"Mills and I have an interview with Horsetalk this morning." He glanced into the mirror hanging in the hall and smoothed his tie.

"Oh right," Hannah mumbled, her mouth still full of toast as she pulled her riding boots on.

"Who are you riding? Did Ashley say not to ride Wolfie?"

Was that a flash of guilt on his face? Hannah thought.

She nodded. "Tolly. Ashley wanted to see how she went with me."

For just a second a shadow flitted across Henry's face. "OK," he said. "See what you think. It's a shame."

Hannah frowned as she headed out to the yard. What did her dad mean by that? Did he mean Wolfie? Or Tolly? She knew Tolly had been seen by the physio and the vet in the last few weeks, as well as having her teeth done. The Boland ponies received the very best of care, and Henry still used the same vet who had treated his Olympic showjumpers. Hannah wondered if they had been looking for a problem. But Tolly certainly wasn't dangerous, or else no one would be allowed to ride her, not even Ashley.

Grabbing her tack, Hannah spent a few minutes fussing over Tolly. The little mare was so sweet, standing quietly with her pale-orange eyelashes closing in the early-morning sunshine.

A car pulled up outside the house and a smartly dressed young woman hopped out, as well as a man carrying some camera equipment. It had to be the Horsetalk team. Ashley was nowhere to be seen, thank goodness, so it was just her and Tolly. Hannah had never minded if Johno watched her ride – he always put her at ease – but Ashley was so critical.

Leading Tolly out into the yard, Hannah tightened the girth and swung lightly up in the saddle. Although Tolly was a couple of hands higher than Wolfie she was finely built so didn't feel big at all.

"Come on, girl." Hannah nudged her towards the arena. "Let's see what we can do."

Chapter Four

Turning Tolly towards the small cross poles that were set up on the pale sand, Hannah nudged her on and Tolly jumped them perfectly. Hannah felt a wave of satisfaction. Tolly was so responsive, with just the right amount of buzz. Perhaps Tolly needed her way of riding. She'd never admit it out loud, but it always felt good to get one up on Millie. Hopping off, she quickly put all the jumps up, and added a couple of spread poles to them too, before dragging a bright pink and green filler over to place under one of the straight bars.

Tolly stood quietly, waiting for Hannah to finish, and Hannah gave her a hug before remounting. "I think you're perfect," she said, picking the canter back up and circling the arena, before heading to the first jump on the short course, a simple upright of about seventy centimetres. *Sit, sit, sit, quietly in the saddle, reins short and...*

"Agh!"

Tolly's violent run-out was so unexpected, Hannah felt herself hanging in the air for a split second before she scrambled back into the saddle, determined not to fall.

"Oh dear!" She gave the chestnut mare a stroke, before turning round and attempting the jump again, only to have the same thing happen. Three, four times.

Tolly was not going to jump, no matter how positively Hannah rode.

Hannah frowned and brought Tolly to a halt with a reassuring pat. The pony just didn't seem to want to jump. There had been nothing malicious about her refusals; she simply wouldn't go over the fence. Hopping off for the second time, Hannah lowered the jump right back down, so Tolly could step over it if she wanted. Hannah didn't want to jump her any more, but equally she didn't want to finish the session on a bad note. Tolly was still relatively young and Hannah knew it was important for her to maintain her confidence. It paid off. Tolly popped sweetly over the tiny jump a couple of times before Hannah gave her a hug and let her cool off by walking her round on a long rein.

So *that* had been the issue. When Henry had mentioned there being nothing physically wrong, that must have been what he was talking about. But to Hannah it was as clear as day. Tolly just didn't like to jump high!

"Out of Van Di-Marco, and won't jump bigger than a cross pole." A scornful voice made Hannah jump out of her skin as she led Tolly back to her stable. She hadn't realised Ashley was there.

"Who's Van Di-whatsit?"

"He's a *top* Dutch pony stallion," Ashley said. "Normally throws excellent jumpers. So annoying that we ended up with the only dud."

Hannah gave Tolly a hug, feeling super protective of her. She was the sweetest pony, and Ashley was being horrible! "Maybe it will come in time," she said. "Her jump."

But Ashley shook his head. "Nope," he said dismissively. "You can tell. She just doesn't have the aptitude for it. What a waste of good breeding!"

"But her flatwork's really nice!" Hannah protested. "And she's lovely in the stable. And Millie said she's really good out hacking. She's hardly a dud."

"Her flatwork is average." Ashley curled his lip. "And great, a *happy hacker*." He rolled his eyes, his contempt for Tolly clear.

Hannah glared at him. She briefly opened her mouth to argue back, but she knew it was no use.

Hannah had finished putting Tolly away and headed for the cool of the house. She'd made sure she had given her an extra-long groom, chatting away as she worked. Hannah wouldn't mind at all if Tolly was her very own pony. Sure, it was exhilarating jumping the enormous fences on ponies like Wolfie, but she knew Tolly would be perfect in her own way, made for long hacks out, endless hours exploring the moors. Ashley put so much emphasis on their breeding and what they could do, what they could win. He never saw them as just ponies who, like people, were all different. *Tolly is clearly never going to be a prizewinner*, Hannah thought sadly, *so he's put her on the rubbish pile*.

He's given up on her.

"Hi, sweetheart," Hannah's mum called from the kitchen. "Your dad and Millie are still doing the interview. They won't be long. I'm just going to look at this bit of Billy's, see if I can find something that suits him better." Mum never seemed to stop. All the small details of the business were down to her.

Hannah fetched herself a glass of water and sat at the kitchen table. She could hear the interview next door, and it sounded as though it was mostly Millie doing the talking. She idly flicked through a magazine and suddenly her parents' faces beamed out at her from a centre spread. Sometimes she forgot just how well known her parents were. It wasn't even a horsey magazine; it was some sort of glossy lifestyle magazine talking about their "fairy-tale romance". Mum had been Dad's groom years ago, before they'd fallen in love at the Olympic Games and returned with not only two gold medals but a diamond ring on Lucy's finger. Their story had enthralled the horsey set and had added to the celebrity status they held in the showjumping world. Hannah gazed at an old photo of her parents, arm in arm years ago at Hickstead before she and Millie had come along. They looked lighter somehow. Her dad was roaring with laughter and her mum looked so pretty and joyful. Hannah thought she was still beautiful, but there was a sparkle about her in the photo that she hadn't seen for a long time.

The interview was still going on next door. Putting the magazine down, Hannah could hear snippets of it.

"Every pony is given the very best start."

"Homes are so important; we make sure each pony is placed with owners who will be a perfect fit."

"Absolutely. A Boland pony is a quality pony. It's what we pride ourselves on. They go on to represent the yard, and our family name."

That was their motto. *A Boland pony is a quality pony.* Henry Boland had a waiting list of clients who wanted to buy from him. Hannah wondered what he would do with Tolly. OK, she wouldn't win the big jumping prizes, but the right home would be out there for her. Hannah imagined a countryside cottage, a girl who just wanted a pony to love and groom and go and say goodnight to in pyjamas. That would be perfect. That was *her* dream. Remembering the letter she'd written to Wispa's owner, she decided to do the same for Tolly and Wolfie's new owners. She knew Wolfie really well, and although she didn't know Tolly as well, she could explain that the mare wasn't disobedient, just that she didn't want to jump, and how sweet and gentle she was in the stable, and how, according to Millie, she had been perfect out hacking. Grabbing some cream paper with the Boland family crest on the header, Hannah selected a biro and began to write.

She'd almost reached the end of the second letter when the man and woman from Horsetalk walked past the window. "Let us know as soon as possible," she heard the woman call back, and Hannah briefly wondered what Millie had been offered now. There was always some new deal.

Millie burst through the door. She had a full face of make-up, making her look older than she was. "Hannah!" She sounded super giddy.

Hannah put down her pen as Millie skipped over, grinning from ear to ear.

"The most amazing thing," Millie said breathlessly. "Huge! You've got to listen to this! Mum!" Millie opened the kitchen window and yelled across the yard. "Come in!"

Frowning, Hannah stood up. "How was Horsetalk?" she asked, watching as her mum hurried back to the house, a slight look of alarm on her face.

"That's the big news!"

Dad came in holding a champagne bottle. He looked as happy as Millie, and Hannah noted a stack of paperwork in her dad's hands. Hannah looked at her mum, her dad and finally at Millie. "So?" she asked. "What's going on?"

"Horsetalk want us to star in a documentary!"

Hannah screwed up her nose. So *that* was the big news?

"It's amazing, isn't it!" Millie exclaimed, not appearing to notice Hannah didn't seem quite as enthusiastic. "They want to make a six-part series all about the yard! It's going to be called 'Life at Heartwood'."

"O ... K," Hannah said slowly.

"So they'll be following us, you and me," Millie said, "I mean, me mostly, but you as well, to the Young Riders showjumping championships at the end of August, the ones Dad won when he was our age, right, Dad? Like, how we prepare and everything. All the behind-the-scenes stuff."

Hannah shook her head. It didn't make sense. She'd qualified Wolfie for the championships and Millie had qualified a pony called Gem. But both ponies were being sold.

"But Wolfie..." She shook her head. "He's going. I heard about the deposit ... and his video..." Her voice trailed off. No one had actually told *her* anything.

"Isn't he?" A slight glimmer of light appeared.

Henry smiled. "Wolfie's staying," he said, and Hannah's heart leapt.

"He's staying?" She felt a grin spread across her face, the glimmer of light now beaming. They'd all fooled her! Her dad had pretended to sell the little bay, but really they were keeping him for her, having seen how much they'd bonded!

"Until after the championships at the end of August," said Henry, and Hannah felt her stomach drop, though no one appeared to notice. "His new owner isn't experienced enough at that level and they'd like you to take the ride. Then they'll take him on after the show. Horsetalk loved Millie's videos of Wolfie and want to follow him for the documentary."

"But it's mostly about me and Gem," Millie added brightly. "You'll be the sidekicks."

Hannah considered this. She'd have Wolfie for longer, but he still wouldn't be hers to love.

"Perhaps we can get you another pony of your own, one you can keep, once the documentary is over," Henry continued. "I know how sad you were when you outgrew Wispa."

Hannah looked at him quizzically. He didn't meet her gaze.

"I didn't outgrow her," she began, but her mum placed a hand on her arm.

"You were near enough outgrowing her," she said. Her tone was gentle but she was shutting the conversation down. "You would have sooner rather than later. And your own pony again, wouldn't that be something? I promise you can choose whatever you like. One that can stay."

"Hannah," her dad said, "we really need to do this." His eyes trailed over to the sideboard where a stack of brown envelopes sat. "Obviously we'd rather you were on board, but we have already said yes. We can't turn this down, not right now."

Hannah gazed at her family's expectant faces. She *hated* the thought of being filmed. It was bad enough appearing in Millie's videos but the programmes on Horsetalk were a huge deal. They were watched all over the world and attracted the biggest names in the sport. Perhaps she could keep her appearances as minimal as possible. By the sound of it Millie and Gem were the stars of the show. Then she thought about being able to keep a pony. Maybe she could find another Wispa, a pony she could call her very own. One that would stay.

"OK," she said carefully. "I'm in."

"Great!" Her dad clapped his hands together, as if there was never any doubt. "They want to start filming as soon as possible and get as much footage as they can before the championships. So please make sure you're available at all times. And we were thinking we would put Ashley in charge of the ponies. Horse Master, as it's known in filming, so I learned today. He knows them best."

Hannah looked at him, quite taken aback. "No, he doesn't!" she said in a shocked voice. "He doesn't know them at all!"

Not like I do, she thought. *He just sees what they can do, as if they were machines.*

"Hannah." Henry sounded slightly irritated. "I need him in charge. He's not let me down yet. Plus, this series is about the yard, and he's a big part of it."

Hannah knew she couldn't argue. They'd already decided what was happening. She tried to think about the pony potentially waiting for her at the end of all this. If she could just get through the summer, maybe it would be worth it.

Chapter Five

"But you *hate* being filmed!"

Gaby stared at her, open-mouthed. She had walked up the hill with Vanessa's dog Milo and she and Hannah were sitting on the wooden bench overlooking the outdoor arena, watching Millie ride one of the youngsters they had in. For once Millie wasn't filming. *Without a camera to grin into*, Hannah thought, *she actually looks normal*. She was totally engrossed in her work, cantering a circle, bringing the pony back to a trot across the diagonal, before nudging her into canter again with a pat to her neck. Millie was a lovely rider, quiet and gentle with sympathetic hands. She always had been. It was a good job too, Hannah reflected, because she knew her sister would be torn to shreds online otherwise.

"And you heard all that with Wispa," Gaby continued. "How you were going to be able to keep her..."

"I know, I know," Hannah said. "But I think it's different this time. And it's only for the summer. Perhaps it will be worth it."

"Hmmm."

Gaby raised an eyebrow, giving Milo a stroke. Hannah closed her eyes, remembering the day Wispa had left. She and Gaby had tried to hide her in the old barn to stop her being taken away, and when Ashley had finally loaded her along with the letter Hannah had written, Hannah had sobbed and sobbed on Gaby's shoulders.

Suddenly the little mare Millie was riding looked up, ears pricked, and gave a shrill whinny. Hannah looked over and gave a start of horror. Ashley was riding Tolly into the arena. Lean and lanky, Ashley wasn't too heavy for the pony, but he was too long, with his stirrups hanging below Tolly's tummy. His gleaming brown boots were flanked by a pair of spurs and he carried a whip. He wasn't letting Tolly have her head at all, and with some quick transitions and a rein back as Tolly flicked her ears back and forth, Hannah knew he was forcing her to listen to him. She felt a pit of worry grow in her stomach and looked at Gaby, who seemed equally horrified.

Hannah saw Millie stop her own pony and watch Ashley, a look of apprehension on her face as he headed Tolly towards the line of jumps. Tolly jumped the first small one clumsily, sending the poles smashing to the ground, and ran out at the bigger second, just as she had done the day before. Ashley's face hardened and he brought his stick down on her hindquarters with a thwack before pulling his hands in, wheeling her round again. This time Tolly jumped it, knocking the poles. Hannah felt as though the chestnut mare was crying out for Ashley to stop it.

"Millie!" Hannah called over to her sister. "Stop him!"

But her words were lost as Ashley cantered past, then over the next jump, this time with a couple of hard whacks, and then on to the next, a huge upright.

"Get ON!" Ashley growled, digging his spurs into

Tolly's sides, but the little mare swung out to the side, avoiding the jump completely. Ashley gave her a thwack and started to wheel her round, but Hannah was faster. She jumped up and ducked under the arena fence, putting herself in the direct line of the jump. Her hands were shaking with anger, her heart racing.

Ashley looked furious as he swung the sweet mare away. "She needs to be told," he said. "You were letting her get away with it."

"Away with what?" Hannah shouted at him. "She doesn't want to jump! She didn't enjoy one bit of that; she only did it because you were forcing her! You can't make her jump any more."

Ashley rolled his eyes, nudging Tolly back towards the gate. "I give up with her anyway. It's useless." As he left the arena he called back over one shoulder. "You're too soft. She's taking the mickey. If you go to any top yard, they'd say the same thing."

"Well, go to one then," Hannah retorted sharply, and Ashley glared at her.

"I wish," he spat, and slammed the gate shut.

Hannah looked desperately at her sister. If anyone could back her up, Millie could. Ashley seemed to have a smidge more respect for her.

"Millie!" Hannah pleaded. "Go after him and tell him! Tell him how wrong that was!"

But Millie just shook her head, her expression unreadable. "He's a harder rider than you, Hannah," she said, "but he didn't hurt her."

"But *you* know what she's like," Hannah said, close to tears now. "You've ridden her more than me. You know she doesn't want to jump."

Millie opened her mouth as if to say something, and Hannah knew her sister agreed with her, but then she shook her head. "I think Ashley was right; she probably is pushing the boundaries a bit. Maybe she sees us as a bit of a soft touch. Perhaps she was seeing what she could get away with. I'm sure Ashley was just trying to help her sale," she added, as if that was supposed to make Hannah feel better. "I promise you she'll be OK."

Hannah wondered if Millie was trying to convince herself of this too.

Gaby and Milo joined Hannah. Gaby gave Millie a look, her eyes narrowed, but Millie didn't seem to notice, nudging on the pony she'd been riding as if nothing had happened. But Hannah couldn't forget the way Tolly had looked as Ashley had jumped her.

"He's got way worse!" Gaby sounded incredulous.

"Why doesn't your sister say anything to him? You have to tell your mum and dad."

"Yes, he has," Hannah said miserably. "But Mum and Dad don't listen! As far as they're concerned, Ashley can do no wrong."

Gaby shook her head. "What a mess," she said, and Hannah wasn't sure if she was talking to Hannah or herself. "OK, well, I'm off. Going to see Vanessa."

"OK," Hannah said awkwardly. Gaby hadn't been there long. "I'll see you soon?"

Gaby nodded and set off with Milo, and Hannah thought about Vanessa's welcoming cosy yard just down the hill. It was the complete opposite of their yard right now.

Later that afternoon, Hannah stood with Tolly in her stable, trying to soothe away her horrible ride. The little mare seemed subdued at first, barely responding as Hannah fussed and patted her, until gradually she gave her a nudge, pricking her ears forward at last. Hannah placed her arms round the kind pony, closing her eyes. Gaby saw it, and Hannah did too. Why didn't her family see what she did?

A couple of days later, Vanessa pulled into the yard with her car and trailer.

Henry gave her a wave. "Hello, Vanessa," he said warmly. "Have you been following the dressage in Germany?"

"Oh yes!" Vanessa said enthusiastically. "That young rider, Serena, she's doing ever so well, isn't she? Beautiful freestyle. One to watch for the Olympics, I think."

"I agree," Henry said. "Great to see such an exciting up-and-coming GB team."

Henry and Vanessa could talk for hours about horses and competing. She was one of the few people Hannah ever saw her dad chat with freely.

"Here we are," Vanessa said to the beautiful horse peering out of the trailer, as she pulled the side ramp down. "Ready for your examination?"

Diego walked happily down the ramp and on to the yard.

"He looks so good," Hannah said. She looked for Gaby in the passenger seat, but there was no sign of her friend.

"Thanks, Hannah," Vanessa said, smiling. "I'm so nervous. Let's just hope everything has been worth it."

During all the months of box rest and walks out in hand, building Diego's strength back up, Vanessa had been so worried. She'd given up so much to get him through rehab and to pay the vet bills.

"Right then." Vanessa took a deep breath as a car pulled up and a smiley young woman, Vanessa's vet, hopped out. Vanessa gave Diego's lead rope a gentle tug, heading towards the arena. "Here we go!"

Hannah watched as the vet went through her examination. Vanessa lunged Diego on both reins in the school, before trotting him up and down the concrete walkway just outside. Ashley walked past with a wheelbarrow and paused. Hannah hadn't spoken to him since the incident with Tolly and felt herself bristle.

"He's still here then," Ashley said. "That horse."

"Yes, and I think Vanessa deserves a medal," Hannah said firmly. "All those months getting him right."

"Hmm," Ashley said. "Bet she's regretting not selling him when she had the chance."

Hannah knew Vanessa had been asked countless times whether she would sell the beautiful dressage horse. Although he was older, he was a schoolmaster, and would have no doubt gone on to win lots more at a lower level. As fate would have it, he was injured a few weeks after Vanessa had received the biggest offer yet.

"Maybe some things are more important than money," Hannah said.

"Oh, Hannah." Ashley rolled his eyes. "Of course *you* can say that. You live in a fairy-tale world. No idea about business."

Vanessa waved and put her thumbs up from where she was standing in the arena, and Hannah didn't have a chance to reply to Ashley. He stalked off.

"It's good news!" Vanessa called, and Hannah waved back, feeling a warm glow. Diego was going to be OK. Vanessa's love and dedication had seen him through the worst. She'd believed in him. Hannah may not completely understand business, but she did understand the love for a horse. Ashley didn't understand at all!

"You really meant it when you said right away!"

Hannah looked around the yard. Everything looked even tidier than normal and some hanging baskets had been added, overflowing with flowers. A couple of black vans were parked up by the horsebox and a team of people were milling around.

"Absolutely!" Millie said brightly. "We're all going to do an intro today." She looked Hannah up and down. "Have you even brushed your hair? Han, I did *tell* you this was happening."

"Yes," Hannah muttered, not quite sure if she had or not. Millie had told her that the film crew wanted to see them in their normal everyday attire, so she'd taken that quite literally and was in her navy jodhs and a T-shirt that might have once been Jenson's.

Millie rolled her eyes. "Well, it's a real-life thing, I guess," she said. "Anyway, we've got no time to sort it. You're riding Wolfie. Come on."

Hannah tacked Wolfie up and led him into the cobbled yard, suddenly aware that she was being filmed. Freddie was there too, doing something for Millie's channel. He looked a bit worried, as if he wasn't sure where he should stand. Normally it was just him and Millie.

"Don't worry," a blond man holding a clipboard said to Hannah, "just act like we're not here. We're going to film you doing your day-to-day bits, and when we want you to come and talk to us, we'll let you know. I'm Logan," he added, "and that's Ann-Marie." He pointed out a woman who had her dark hair piled up on her head and secured with a tortoiseshell clip. "She's director. The big chief."

"OK," Hannah said, self-consciously swinging herself up into the saddle and giving Wolfie a big pat. It felt so good to be back on him! As she rode the little gelding round the arena, walking, trotting and cantering on both reins, the camera started to melt away and it was just her and Wolfie.

Wolfie loved to jump and he was soon flying over the coloured fences, a total contrast to Tolly. Hannah could just feel it in Wolfie: how much he enjoyed it, the way his ears pricked and he danced, bouncing on the spot as they turned the corners, before leaping the big jumps as if they were nothing. She thought of Ashley whipping Tolly into the jumps. You shouldn't have to force them that much, she thought, the familiar bubble of anger rising up again. Not if they don't want to.

"That was great, Hannah, thanks."

Logan seemed happy with the footage and Hannah felt herself relax. Maybe this wasn't so bad after all!

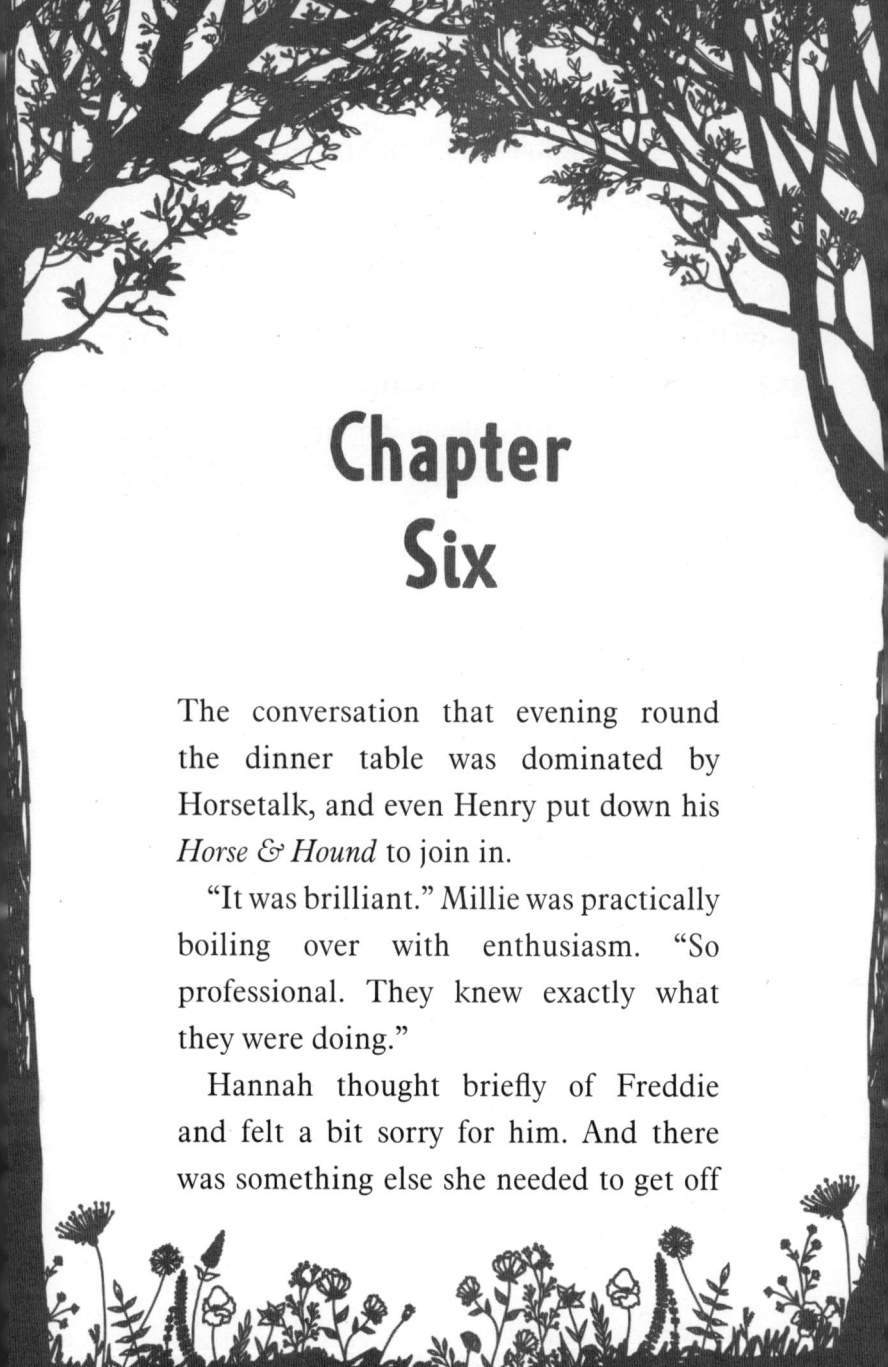

Chapter Six

The conversation that evening round the dinner table was dominated by Horsetalk, and even Henry put down his *Horse & Hound* to join in.

"It was brilliant." Millie was practically boiling over with enthusiasm. "So professional. They knew exactly what they were doing."

Hannah thought briefly of Freddie and felt a bit sorry for him. And there was something else she needed to get off her chest.

"Will they be filming Ashley?" she asked, and her dad shrugged.

"Of course," he answered. "He's head groom. Why wouldn't they?"

"Riding?" Hannah continued, and Henry raised an eyebrow.

"If he's needed to," he said. "Why do you ask?"

"What if he's hard on the horses?" Hannah persisted. "How would that look? He wasn't very kind to Tolly yesterday."

"Look," Henry said, "I know he rides differently to you. But he's very, very good at his job, and I'm sure he'll remain professional. And I heard about Tolly. He does get results, Hannah; he has to push them a bit."

Hannah knew her dad was putting a stop to the conversation.

"Anyway," Henry said, "what about tomorrow? Are they back filming?"

Millie nodded, her mouth full of pasta. "Yep," she said once she'd finished. "They want to shoot some intro-type stuff, like panoramic views of the moors and some drone shots. Oh, and they want a really nice pony under the cherry tree in the courtyard."

"What about Tolly?" Hannah suggested. "She's so

pretty." She wanted to give the sweet chestnut her time to shine.

"Probably not the one to use," Dad said, and shifted in his seat. A slight frown momentarily creased his brow. "Tolly's off tomorrow. Ashley's found her a good home. Friend of a friend."

Hannah looked at him, confused. When ponies were sold there were often several visits. Sometimes people brought their trainers with them or sponsors. She couldn't recall seeing anyone visit for Tolly. "Oh," she said, feeling disappointed. "Did she sell unseen then?"

"She did." Henry clapped his hands together, seemed to compose himself and gave her a big smile. "You know how the market is! It's not unusual, especially if there's travel involved. And she was recommended by Ashley. She didn't sell for a lot, but I think the right home is more important, isn't it? As long as she's happy."

Hannah thought about the home she'd dreamed up for Tolly, the cute countryside cottage, plenty of great hacking, a girl who would have new brushes and rugs waiting for her. Her heart softened slightly. Maybe she had her dad wrong, thinking he was all about the profit. She felt pleased, as if she had proved Gaby wrong.

"So who bought her? What's their name?" Hannah asked. "She'd be perfect in a hacking home."

"Yes, exactly!" Henry replied brightly. "She'll be just fine. And we've got a really exciting new youngster joining us the day after next. He's come over from Germany and used to being stabled so I need some space. Got the makings of a real star."

He hadn't answered her question, Hannah thought. His mind was already on the next money-spinner. Hannah remembered Millie's words in the Horsetalk interview, about how each pony was carefully placed with their new owners. Tolly would have a nice home waiting, wouldn't she?

Hannah couldn't shake her feeling of unease the next day. She was back out in the yard long before her alarm went off and let her chickens out of their coop, counting them one by one as they clucked and shook their feathers in the early-morning sunlight. From the corner of her eye she saw Ashley head over to the barn where the horsebox was kept. A few minutes later, he swung his truck into the yard. He clearly wasn't taking the big blue horsebox with BOLAND SHOWJUMPERS on the side. Instead, he had attached the old green trailer to his truck. He jumped out and lowered the back ramp.

Letting herself out of the chickens' enclosure, Hannah hurried over to the stables. Ashley was leading Tolly out of her stable towards the ramp.

"Wait!" Hannah cried. "Is she going now?"

Ashley barely glanced at her. "Thought it best I got her out of the way before the film crew comes back. She *is* sold, you know."

"But you haven't put any leg bandages on," Hannah pointed out. Then she had a thought. "And wouldn't it be good to have her on film? Show what we do, her going off to her new home?"

Ashley gave a short laugh. "Save that for something like Wolfie."

Hannah felt a flash of anger. "Let me at least get her some leg bandages," she said. "Why isn't she going in the horsebox?"

"The film crew wanted the horsebox in a shot today." Ashley shrugged. "And I've got to go down some narrow lanes. Easier this way."

Ashley waited for Hannah to fasten some blue travel bandages on Tolly's slim chestnut legs. As Hannah fastened the last Velcro strap, the little mare breathed into her hair and Hannah felt a tug in her heart.

"I hope you'll be happy at your new home." She stood up and hugged Tolly. "Dad said it was a good place."

"Course it is," Ashley said. "But there won't be a home at all if I'm late. Come on, let me get her loaded."

"Will you take a photo of her?" Hannah asked. "At her new home?"

Ashley rolled his eyes. "OK," he said. "If I must."

Then she remembered something else: the letter she had written. Sprinting back to the kitchen, she grabbed it from her pile of books and handed it to Ashley.

"Here you go," she said. "Can you give this to her new owners?"

Ashley took it and stuffed it in the pocket of his breeches. "OK," he said. "Right, I do have to go."

Hannah watched as the chestnut pony obediently followed Ashley up the ramp and stood quietly as she was tied up. As Ashley pushed the back ramp up behind her, obscuring her from Hannah's view, her feeling of unease grew stronger. She watched the truck and trailer pull out of the gates and down the lane. It wasn't unusual for Ashley to deliver ponies, but something felt different this time. Something felt wrong.

❁ ❃ ❁

Ashley was back a couple of hours later. Hannah felt a wave of sadness as she saw the empty trailer. She watched her dad stroll over and the two men had a brief exchange before Henry clapped Ashley on the back. Seeing Hannah, Ashley headed over and dug his phone out from his pocket.

"Photo as requested," he said in a slightly mocking way, holding the screen so Hannah could see. There was little Tolly, outside a pleasant-looking wooden stable block with blue doors. Hannah could see some fields in the background, and Tolly looked alert but not upset. "See?"

Hannah nodded. "OK," she said, feeling better. She didn't like Ashley, and hated the way he rode, but at least Tolly had a nice home. She wished she could see her new owner. Just get a feel for who they were. Tolly deserved someone who would love her for exactly who she was…

❁ ❃ ❁

Hannah was still thinking about Tolly as filming began with Logan and Ann-Marie. Luckily the crew only needed her for a short while. All she had to do was smile and say, "Hi, I'm Hannah Boland, and I'm thirteen years old." Then she had to stand outside Wolfie's stable while the little bay nuzzled her palm and say a few words about him. Logan was patient enough, but she could tell he was becoming exasperated when Hannah made a few mistakes, forgetting the words, stumbling over her own name and looking into the wrong camera. She breathed a sigh of relief when he told her they had what they needed. Unlike Millie, who was a natural, Hannah just felt awkward and clumsy.

She watched as Millie did her bit in one smooth take, standing outside Gem's stable. She wore her brightest smile and patted the pony as she chatted. Freddie took some photos.

"This would be a great behind-the-scenes bit." He smiled at Hannah, showing her the stills. His camera was in a battered leather suitcase that had belonged to his grandad. He'd told Hannah once that he was saving up for new equipment but that it was really expensive, even the camera bags. Although she didn't really take much interest in what Freddie did for Millie, Hannah thought he was super talented. She treasured a head shot he'd taken of Wispa one frosty day, capturing all of her wild Welsh beauty.

"Actually, mate." Logan waved a hand. "Can you just stand back a bit? Better if you're away from the filming. We'll have loads of photos if you want one."

Freddie looked a bit startled but stepped back obediently. Hannah decided she didn't like Logan.

For the next bit Ashley joined Millie. He'd changed into a plaid shirt and brown breeches. Logan trained the camera on the pair of them and gave a thumbs up.

"This is Ashley," Millie said in a tinkly voice. "Ashley is like family to us. He was born and brought up here at Heartwood, and we couldn't do this without him."

"I love my job here, but it's more like a way of life for me," Ashley said, smiling widely for the camera. Hannah raised an eyebrow. His voice sounded completely false; she'd never seen him grin like that. "I love seeing the variety of ponies we have through the gates. Each one is so different, and each one is special in its own way. Our job is to find out where the pony will shine, so we can give it the best future at the right home. It's so rewarding. We treat each pony with kindness and allow them to flourish. From the happy hackers to the Horse of the Year Show winners, they're all equally important."

Hannah looked at Millie and then back at Ashley, not quite believing what she was hearing. Was this the same Ashley who had dismissed Tolly as a dud, who had scorned her, then forced her to jump despite her reluctance? The same Ashley who had rolled his eyes at Vanessa and Diego? Millie was smiling blandly and everyone looked really pleased, but Hannah felt a bubble of anger grow inside her.

"Millie!" Hannah grabbed her sister's arm as she walked away from the stable. Ashley had snapped back into his normal sullen glare as soon as the filming had stopped and hurried off.

"Why did you let Ashley say what he said?" Hannah hissed, aware that Logan was still hovering nearby. "It's not true!"

"Shh!" Millie frowned and walked further away from Logan. "It is true. I know you and Ashley don't see eye to eye, but that's because you're not running the business." She got her phone out and started to scroll down the screen, not looking at Hannah. "You have to be tough sometimes."

"Ashley's not running the business either!" Hannah exclaimed. "Dad is!"

"And Dad trusts Ashley." Millie shrugged. "Look, he was a little hard on Tolly, but that's just how he is."

"And don't you want to know where Tolly's gone?" Hannah said. "Dad didn't even seem to know the new owner's name."

Millie made a face. "She'll be fine," she said. "The trouble with you, Hannah, is you've never forgiven anyone for Wispa going." Hannah winced. "We *have* to sell ponies, that's what we do. And we have to put our best self out there in order to do it." She was speaking very slowly, as if explaining things to a small child. "Look, can you help me pack? I've got some stuff to put on the lorry."

Hannah sighed. "Sure." She slung Millie's show kit bag on her shoulder and picked up Gem's grooming kit, muttering under her breath. Millie and Gem were due to head off early the next morning to a big showjumping class that the film crew were also going along to, which meant a day free for Hannah. Happily it coincided with the day of the festival. Hannah couldn't wait for her day with Gaby and Jenson away from it all.

Placing the holdall down in the living area, Hannah's tummy rumbled, and her eyes lit upon the drawer where all the documents, and sweets, were usually kept for journeys. The drawer was crammed full and as she pulled out a pink-and-white striped bag a handful of paper spilled out alongside it. Her heart thudded as she spotted a crumpled envelope that had been stuffed underneath all the paperwork.

It was her writing on the front.

Wispa's new owner.

Wispa had been gone for just over five months. The new owners would never know about the tea, or the bowing, or her funny hatred of red buckets – none of it. Both her dad and Ashley had known about the letter. She could believe Ashley would forget. But Dad? Was that how little her and Wispa's relationship mattered to him?

She thought about the letter Ashley had put into his pocket for Tolly. She bet that hadn't been delivered either.

Hannah choked back a furious sob and screwed the envelope up into a tight ball.

Chapter Seven

Hannah felt like a zombie as she waited at the bus stop with Jenson and Gaby. She'd barely slept a wink, and when she had she'd slept fitfully, dreaming about the lorry taking Wispa away. It was too late now to get the letter to Wispa's new owners. They would have got to know her by now, but in a completely different way.

Hannah's phone gave a ping. Millie had just posted a photograph and must have tagged her. She pulled her phone out and glared at it. She was so sick of it all.

"I don't even want to read this!" she exclaimed, putting her head in her hands.

"It can't be that bad, can it?"

Reaching over, Jenson wiggled the phone out of Hannah's grip, and with an utterance of frustration Hannah let him take it, sliding back down on to the bench and folding her arms. She couldn't bear to look at the photo anyway: Millie leaning down from the saddle and hugging a pretty dun pony. Gaby was eating a bag of crisps next to her, listening intently.

"*I'm so excited to tell you some amazing news,*" Jenson read the words from the screen, copying Millie's chirpy voice. "*You're going to love it! But first, here's an update on Saffie, one of the ponies we have in for sale at the moment. Isn't she the sweetest? Ashley has been working really hard on her pole work, and, guys, I've just had the nicest hack. We cantered through a gorgeous flower meadow. What pony activities do you like doing best in summer?*"

Jenson passed the phone back and Hannah glared at her sister in the image. She hadn't been hacking today. What was she on about?

Jenson shrugged, almost absent-mindedly taking a crisp from Gaby's bag. "Looks like all Millie's other posts. Ponies, sunshine, blah, blah."

Gaby swatted his hand away from the crisps. "Jenson's right, it does," she said. "All perfect, as per." There was a distinct edge to her voice.

Hannah scrolled down the screen. The photo was gaining tens of likes by the second, mostly from girls around her age. The comments on Millie's posts were all heart eyes and smiley faces, and loads of *You're amazing, Millie. I look up to you so much!* and *Aw, Saffie is so gorgeous. I wish she was mine!* Hannah could feel her annoyance building again, but it was more than that this time. It was a growing sense of realisation. She didn't feel like defending her family any more.

"You saw what I saw, didn't you?" she said miserably to her friend. "How Ashley rode Tolly in the school, how Millie just dismissed it."

"I did," Gaby said carefully.

"It's all so ... *fake*! All of them. And now, with the filming, they're making me a part of it. It makes me want to scream."

Looking back at Millie's photo, Hannah lifted her arm to chuck her phone to the floor and let the screen crack into a million pieces. Only the thought that she wouldn't be able to replace it stopped her. Millie's perfect snapshot was *putting their best selves out there*, as she put it, but Hannah was starting to realise what lay beneath.

It felt strange being in town a short while later. Hannah only rarely left Heartwood – to go to horse shows or school. There was an excited buzz on the streets as hordes of teenagers, painted with glitter and wearing their wildest festival gear, headed for the big park. Hannah could hear the distant thrum of music. Getting swept up in the crowds, she felt a surge of happiness. This was just what she needed after the last twenty-four hours.

"Oh no!" Gaby shouted in dismay as they reached the edge of the parkland. "My shoe!"

One of the straps on Gaby's sandal had snapped. She hopped along, trying to keep her balance. The friends stumbled away from the crowd to the shade of one of the ancient oaks so Gaby could try to fix it. Hannah waited as her friend examined the buckle and then started to repair it with a hair band from her bag.

The park was huge, and the festival was only in one part of it. Looking around, Hannah stopped as something caught her eye. Every hair on her neck stood up. There was something over there up on the verge. It was the prettiest wagon painted red and green, with a thin plume of smoke rising from it, and a couple of ponies grazing next to it. It was the most beautiful, calm scene, a total contrast to the vibrant chaos of the festival crowd.

Feeling an almost magnetic pull, Hannah walked towards it. It was like someone else had control of her feet. Next to a sweet-looking black and white cob stood a grey mare. Hannah looked at her and the mare looked back, lifting her head and staring with dull eyes. Her look was like lightning, striking right into Hannah's heart.

"Hannah?" Gaby called as Hannah ran away from the crowd, towards the wagon and the pony. The mare watched her the whole time. She was thin, her coat rough, and her tail yellow with grease and dirt, but Hannah had been around horses long enough to recognise a really beautiful pony. About fourteen hands, she looked like a Connemara and had the softest eyes. Hannah had never seen the pony in her life as far as she knew, but she seemed so familiar. It was the oddest feeling, like *déjà vu*.

"Hey." Hannah stretched out an upturned hand and let the mare breathe over it, feeling the whiskers tickle her skin. How she longed to wash and comb out that raggedy mane, to apply some purple shampoo to her stained coat to bring out the lustrous white, and to put her in one of Heartwood's soft fleece head collars.

"Hannah!" Gaby had mended her shoe and had now caught up with her, Jenson running alongside.

"What are you doing?" Gaby said, and then looked at the pony. "Oh." Her face softened.

A man appeared, making them all jump, and glared at them. "If you've come to tell me the pony is too thin, I've had a dozen of you festivalgoers already today calling the RSPCA and all sorts," he said in a cross voice. "I *know* she looks terrible. I've just bought her from an auction. She was headed off to who knows where until I intervened."

Hannah looked at the man and back at the ponies. The other pony was rounded and shiny and healthy-looking, a stark contrast to the grey. Hannah decided he was telling the truth. "I'm sorry,' she mumbled. "It's just that…" She couldn't explain it. "I feel like I know her from somewhere."

The mare edged closer, and Hannah stretched out her hand again. The pony sniffed it cautiously, whispering her lovely warm breath on Hannah's palm. Looking into her eyes, Hannah felt the same electric surge. The pony spoke to her in a way no pony had ever done.

Gaby tugged her arm. "Han," she said, "what are you doing? We're going to miss the first band, and we need to get to the front row for Lulabella." She clearly thought Hannah had taken leave of her senses. "She's just been rescued. I'm sure she's safe now."

But the man seemed to soften slightly. "I've got to say," he said, "that's the least frightened I've seen her since I bought her. She's been terrified of her own shadow: won't approach anyone, won't let anyone approach her. She's just totally shut down until now. Maybe you do know her. Or perhaps you did in another life."

"What was going to happen to her?" Hannah asked.

"I've a couple of guesses and neither of them are nice. But in the end mine was the only bid. I needed another pony. I've got Dallas there –" he gestured at the black and white pony – "but I want to share his load. I must have been feeling sentimental. I shouldn't have bought her really; she wasn't what I was looking for. She's a quality pony, but she won't be right for me on the road. Dallas is solid, nothing will spook him. She's nervy. You can just tell."

"What will you do with her?" Gaby asked. She was

no longer trying to pull Hannah away. Even Jenson was listening intently.

"Feed her up, gain some trust back." The man shrugged. "But I'll need to sell her before winter. I'll find her the right home, someone who'll love her for her."

"I'll buy her," Hannah said, before she could stop herself. "I've got some money." She quickly calculated. She'd been saving birthday and Christmas money for ages and had some show winnings. It was all safe in her bank account.

"I have two hundred and fifty that I can give you today." She heard her voice falter with nerves.

Gaby put her hand over Hannah's and unspoken words passed between them. Hannah knew what Gaby was thinking, and vice versa, and this was no exception. Gaby turned to the man. "I know it sounds crazy, but *would* you sell her?"

The man laughed. "You seem nice kids," he said. "But you're just kids."

Hannah took a deep breath. She hated using the family name, but she had to this time. "Do you know Henry Boland?" she asked, and the man nodded.

"Showjumper, right?"

Hannah nodded. "He's my dad," she explained.

"I'm Hannah. I live at Heartwood Stables. I can promise you she'll have a good home."

The man looked thoughtful, and his face hardened slightly.

"Hannah, my name's Rollo. I can strike a deal with you," he said. "Four hundred and she's yours."

Hannah felt her heart plummet. How was she going to magic up the rest of the money?

"I can't do that," she said miserably, and Rollo shrugged.

"I'm not looking to make a profit, but I have to make my money back. I can't give her away," he said matter-of-factly. "I won't survive otherwise. Look, I'm moving on tomorrow, not sure where yet, but probably north. I can take her with me or I can sell her to you today. I don't have a phone, so I won't be able to keep in touch."

"I can do the rest," Jenson said, and Hannah turned to him in shock. Jenson had a part-time job in the village newsagent's, but Hannah knew he had been saving hard for an expensive bit of camera equipment.

Hannah shook her head, drawing Jenson aside. "No," she whispered. "Your camera?"

But Jenson shrugged. "Probably won't get me any more views," he said wryly. "And it's kind of cool, isn't it? Buying a random pony? Your mum and dad are going to kill you, and then kill me and Gabs probably."

Hannah's blood ran cold. In just a few minutes not only had she totally forgotten the festival, but she had somehow totally forgotten her family too. It was like the pony had put her under a spell. Every part of her was yearning to get her home, and she hadn't really thought beyond that. But then she remembered finding the undelivered letter. The way her parents had overlooked her to take Ashley's opinion, how they glossed over cruel things like Ashley's treatment of Tolly. So what if everyone was cross? She felt an odd mixture of nerves and exhilaration.

Hannah turned back to Rollo and shook his rough, weather-worn hand.

"Four hundred," she said. "Deal."

Chapter Eight

"Is there nothing you can do?"

"No," the bank clerk said firmly. "I'm sorry. We've got a strict policy; you can only withdraw fifty pounds at a time from young person's savers. That's why the machine wouldn't let you take out more. Any more than fifty pounds and we need advance notice." He peered at them, taking in their festival clothes, Jenson's skateboard and Gaby's glittered eyelids. Hannah knew he was thinking the worst.

"I don't have advance notice." She felt her eyes swim with tears, but she knew it was no use. "I don't have any time at all!"

"I'm sorry, but it's the rules, I'm afraid." He clearly thought the teenagers were trying it on.

"That's it!" Hannah stumbled into the bright sunshine of the high street. Everything was blurry. "I've lost her." She looked at her friends, tears streaming down her cheeks. "I know you think I'm crazy," she said. "But I feel like I've seen her before. I have to get her. I don't know why, but I've never felt anything like this."

Then she looked down. "I'm so sorry," she mumbled. "The festival. I've ruined the day for you."

Gaby smiled. "I don't know," she said. "You're normally the sensible one, Han. This is cool, I think. An adventure."

Hannah sniffed. "But we can't buy her."

"Or … I've got an idea," Gaby said. She dug out her phone and dialled. "Hi, Vanessa –" she made a thumbs-up sign to Hannah – "no, no, we're all good. No, not at the festival. We … um … we've sort of bought a pony. Yep, really. And we need your help."

The sight of Vanessa's black estate and trailer pulling

up to the verge was the most welcome thing Hannah had ever seen. To get here so quickly Vanessa must have dropped what she was doing, hitched up her trailer and got on the road. Hannah wondered what her own parents would have done. Probably wanted to know the pony's breeding or competition record first. Actually they would have gone wild at her. She tried to push her parents out of her mind, still not quite sure how she was going to tell them. But it was exciting too.

Vanessa strode across the grass, her purple shirt tucked into tie-dye shorts. "OK," she said. "Do you want to tell me what's going on?"

"I promise you I'll give you the money as soon as I can," Hannah repeated. "I have to put a request in to the bank and then they'll do it and then I'll cycle over. I promise…"

But Vanessa placed a hand on her arm. "It's OK," she said gently. "I know you will. I also know you well enough to know you'd only do something like this if you really felt you had to." She looked over at the little mare next to the black and white pony. Hannah wondered how many times she'd been bought and sold.

Rollo took the money, counting each note in turn, before untying the mare. There was something about the way he patted her neck that confirmed he was a good person, Hannah thought. He'd saved the pony in the first place.

"What's her name?" she asked, and Rollo shrugged.

"She was just 'grey mare' in the schedule," he said, and it reminded Hannah of Ashley. "And I wanted to get to know her better before giving her a proper name, something that suits her. Here's a passport."

Hannah flicked through the document. She was unregistered, with no name and of unknown breeding. Her date of birth, just the year, made her nine years of age. *Her whole life ahead of her*, Hannah thought. *And who knows what would have happened!*

"That's unusual." Vanessa raised an eyebrow. "No details at all? She's a Connemara through and through."

"You know as well as I do that's not her real passport," Rollo said.

Hannah gaped at him. "Isn't that illegal?"

He gave a short sharp laugh. "Of course it's illegal, and that's not even the worst of it. Funny how they judge *me*, and yet all this is going on." Then he smiled, handing the rope over to Hannah. "I'm a big believer in fate," he said. "You seem to know each other, or maybe you were just meant to find each other. I've never seen anything like it before. Here. She's yours. She's been through it, this one. Her eyes tell the story."

"Thank you for saving her," said Hannah. "I won't let her, or you, down."

The little grey loaded quietly and obediently, trembling slightly. She had no fight left in her. Hannah tied her up, thanking Vanessa for the sweet-smelling hay net she had tied up in preparation.

She placed her forehead against the pony's. "I'll call you Bella," she whispered. "After the band we were supposed to see today." The festival felt a million miles away now. Hannah closed her eyes, feeling the pony's soft coat against her own skin. She couldn't shake the feeling she'd had earlier. This had been written in the stars somehow. Even Rollo, a total stranger, had agreed. Bella was coming home to Heartwood. It was meant to be.

It was mid-afternoon when Vanessa's car and trailer pulled up the drive. The sun was high in the sky, blazing down on the yellowing lawn. The yard was deserted, and a couple of the ponies looked over their doors with pricked ears, but most just remained in the cool shadows of their stables. Trailers and lorries coming and going was nothing exciting.

Hannah breathed a sigh of relief as she clocked the empty space where the Boland lorry usually sat. Her parents and Millie were still at the show with Gem. The classes could go on for hours, and from a quick look at her phone, Hannah knew Millie was into the jump-off and was waiting to ride again. They had a couple of hours to get Bella settled in, and for Hannah to prepare herself for facing her parents.

"Come on, girl." Hannah lowered the ramp, and Bella gazed out. It was the most alert Hannah had seen her since she'd first spotted her in the park, and the way she held her head, her ears pricked, took her breath away. Despite being too thin, dirty and unkempt, she was the most beautiful pony.

"She's really nice," Jenson said, stretching his long limbs after the journey. "You know me, I don't know a thing about horses, but she's nice. Sort of like she's not real in a way. Like from another world."

Gaby smiled. "I know what you mean. I agree. She's lovely."

"She is." Hannah untied Bella's lead rope. "Come on, girl, this way." She led the little mare down the ramp and across the main stable yard, where there was no room. She was going to make her up a temporary pen in the corner of the open-sided barn, so she was slightly away from the sales ponies. Just in case. Bella walked beside her, keeping up with every stride.

"Like you know where you're going!" Hannah said, laughing, and led her into the stable.

Vanessa needed to get back to check on Diego and Muffin, so after hugging her goodbye Hannah and her friends set to work on Bella's makeshift stable, putting down a clean bed of soft white shavings and hanging up a hay net. Jenson found a spare water bucket and Hannah rooted through the boxes of goodies Millie kept in the tack room to find a head collar and a smart fleece, which she hung up on a nail, ready to use after Bella's first bath.

It was one of the happiest afternoons Hannah had had in ages. Buoyed up by her friends' enthusiasm, she was almost ready to confess to her parents. She heard an engine pulling into the yard and took a deep breath. It was now or never…

"Hannah?"

Not Henry, or Lucy, or Millie. A lanky figure appeared round the corner. Ashley.

"What are you up to?" Ashley's lip was curled. Then he stopped in his tracks, as Bella, alerted by another voice, looked up. For a second, time seemed to stop. Bella looked at Ashley and Ashley looked at Bella, and Hannah felt the tension crackling in the air as he stared open-mouthed at the new arrival.

"What on *earth* have you done, Hannah? What is this?"

Hannah thought about the letter in the horsebox and raised her chin, as if *daring* him to cross her. "She's my new pony. It was my money," she said calmly, squeezing Jenson's hand, remembering how he'd come to the rescue. "And Jenson's. I bought her from a really nice man in Writley Park. He rescued her from a sale!"

"And?" Ashley said, clearly exasperated. "You can't just go buying rescue horses! It's not our problem!"

"I know." Hannah stood firm. "It's *my* problem. She's my pony. Our pony." She looked at her friends, who nodded. "You can't tell me what to do!"

Ashley came closer. "I know that," he said crossly. "But she's an old nag, and every stable space is vital to the business. This is the last thing we need."

"Just look at her," said Hannah. "She needs care and a good home. I'll look after her." As she moved aside so Ashley could inspect Bella, she was sure his expression changed. His eyes flashed black, and he made the oddest face for a split second. Hannah wondered if Bella's condition had actually got to him; maybe he felt sorry for the sweet mare.

But then Ashley's face was blank again. "Hannah," he said, his voice flat, "you can't keep her."

"Why?"

Before Ashley could answer, Millie marched round the corner, still in her white competition breeches and custom-made pink-and-white-striped show shirt, carrying an enormous "first place" rosette in one hand and leading a tired but content-looking Gem. Hannah hadn't even heard the lorry come back. Henry and Lucy followed her, laughing and chatting loudly. Hannah knew it had been a big-money class.

"Oh, Han, you should have been there," Millie babbled. "We won by half a second! Gem was amazing – so fast. We did this turn and took the last from one stride out, and, you'll never guess what, Finesse Horseboxes approached me afterwards, wanting to keep in touch about sponsorship, and—" She stopped as she noticed the scene in front of her.

"Oh!" she said, her face softened with surprise. "Who's this? This surely isn't the youngster from Germany?"

Ashley folded his arms. "You'd better ask Hannah,"

win in front of the film crew and the possibility of sponsorship from a posh horsebox company seemed to have softened the blow, but Henry didn't look at all impressed.

"Just look at her, Dad. She needed a home, someone who loves her. Rollo said—"

"Oh for goodness' sake, Hannah, you don't know this Rollo from Adam," her dad snapped, cutting her off. He climbed over the hurdles and then seemed to wince as he took in Bella's full body, thin and ragged. "Well, looking like that, she's stuck here for a bit, at least until she looks better."

"Forever," Hannah corrected him, and her dad frowned.

"Hannah, you don't know anything about her by the sounds of it. She could be dangerous, ill, anything. Let's just get through these next few days. Actually we need to get through the rest of this day to start with. The film crew are on their way over. I can't deal with this now."

Hannah's mum gave her a hug, but it was pretty resigned. "We'll think it over."

"I'm sorry, Mum," Hannah said. "I just fell in love. And what Rollo told me about the sale sounded horrible. I used my own money from birthdays and

Christmas. She wasn't that much."

She tried to sound casual. It was a huge amount to her, but she knew for a fact her dad had sold ponies in the past with two zeroes added on to Bella's price.

"I remember going to an auction once," said Lucy. "Not a smart one like for the thoroughbreds. How I didn't go home with every pony there, I don't know. So I do understand. *Sort* of." She raised one eyebrow, but Hannah knew she'd got off lightly. For now.

Henry Boland walked right the way round the mare, looking her up and down. Hannah held her breath, wondering what he was thinking. His face had softened very slightly.

"She's actually a nice sort," Henry remarked. "She needs feeding up, and she's lacking muscle. She may have been cheap, Hannah, but she'll cost us a bit to feed to get her back to health." He paused. "You can see a good pony there underneath. Proper Connemara type. Wonder what happened to her, poor thing."

He looked at Bella again, frowning. "She seems familiar."

Hannah gave a start, remembering seeing Bella for the first time in the park. How it was like she had awoken some long-forgotten memory.

Ashley snorted. He'd been silent until now, arms

folded. "That's because grey Connies are two a penny. They're as common as anything."

"Yes." Henry shook his head. "I'm sure you're right."

Hannah noticed Ashley hadn't said anything to her in front of her mum and dad about not keeping the pony. Bella took a step towards the hurdles, nearer to Ashley, the closest she'd got so far and then it was as if she realised something within. Her head flew up in alarm as she backed away, eyes rolling, body quivering. Hannah drew her in close, placing a hand on her neck in a protective manner. Bella was certainly a good judge of character!

There was a rumble of tyres as the film crew arrived at the gate. They had followed the horsebox home to get Millie's post-show interview.

"Oh no," Henry said, sounding flustered, "they're here." He looked at Hannah. "Just keep her in this pen," he said, gesturing at Bella.

Hannah watched as Millie hurried over to greet the crew, her ponytail still perfectly bouncy even after being squished under a riding hat, and breathed a sigh of relief, the heat taken off her.

Ann-Marie and Logan unloaded their kit and as they crossed the yard, Ann-Marie seemed to pause as she passed Bella's pen in the barn. "Oh!" she said. "Is this the new pony? Ashley said he was arriving today." Her eyes scanned the little grey mare, and her expression changed. Hannah knew what she was thinking. Bella didn't look good, especially in comparison to the glossy Gem who they'd been filming all day.

"Yeah, but it's not the pony you were told about," Hannah said. "A bit unexpected. More of a rescue really."

"A rescue?" Ann-Marie beamed, and Hannah could practically see the director's mind whirring. "That's exciting! Perhaps I could include her in today's filming? What's her story? How did you find her?"

"Oh," Hannah said, glancing at her dad, who had a slight crease in his brow, for once seeming uncertain about what to do. "Yes, I mean—"

"No." Ashley placed himself between the two of them. "Sorry, Ann-Marie," he said, smoothing back his hair, "but I want to get Gem turned out; she's had a long day. Sorry, but as Horse Master –" and Hannah was sure he smirked as he used his title – "I just think it's really important we stick to schedule. Actually, look –" he gestured towards the main gates where a big blue lorry with INTERNATIONAL TRANSPORT emblazoned on the side was pulling in – "this is the youngster arriving. This is what we *actually* do."

Ann-Marie watched, an excited expression on her face as the most beautiful chestnut pony with a perfect star on his fine forehead was unloaded by the horse transporter team. The pony wore sheepskin-lined travelling boots and a matching head collar and was shining with good health. Ann-Marie seemed to lose interest in Bella. "You're right," she said. "Let's crack on. Maybe another time, Hannah?"

"OK," Hannah said.

Her dad gave her a tight smile, and he and her mum headed over to greet the horse transporter. As Ann-Marie and Ashley went over to where Millie and Gem were waiting for the final bit of filming, Ashley glanced back at her.

His mouth was set firm, his eyes hard. "There won't be another time," he mouthed silently.

Hannah turned away. She wouldn't let Ashley control her. But he seemed genuinely shaken by Bella's arrival. What was his problem?

Ashley made sure Hannah kept Bella away from the main yard. He kept talking about the risk of infectious diseases and general lack of room, but Hannah was glad to keep Bella away from Ashley. It meant she could throw herself into Bella's care, spending every moment she wasn't riding with the sweet grey mare.

For two days Hannah let the little pony graze in the tiny paddock next to the barn, so that she could get settled and start to gain weight. Once Bella seemed calmer, Hannah decided she could give her a bath, enlisting the help of Gaby and Jenson. As she tied Bella up outside the barn and dipped her sponge into a bucket of warm soapy water, Bella's ears pricked up. She stood quietly as the teenagers soaped her coat, watching as the dirt ran out, until the water was gradually clear, lathering up her mane before rinsing her off and combing conditioner through her thick tail. As Bella's white coat started to dry off in the sun, she seemed to sparkle, and Hannah stood back, admiring her handiwork. Bella really was something special.

The next job was to get the vet to check Bella over. There was no record of any vaccinations in her passport, and most likely her teeth would need looking at too. Hannah headed to the house to ask Mum or Dad to ring Alistair at the surgery, as she wasn't allowed to make bookings herself. As she approached the door of the office, she paused. Her parents were deep in conversation. Dad was frowning, and Mum was rubbing the side of her forehead.

"We'll need to make an appointment at the bank," her mum said. "I'll phone the branch tomorrow and ask to see the manager. You'll have to come with me this time, Henry."

Hannah knocked on the open door, and Henry quickly closed the screen.

"Han!" Her mum sounded unnaturally bright. "All OK?"

"Yes," Hannah said, feeling a little unsure. There was a tense atmosphere, despite her mum's smile. "I just wondered if you could ask Alistair to come and check on Bella."

Henry shrugged. "Sure," he said. "If it's not urgent, can it wait a few days?" He smiled. "He's coming early next week anyway, and it saves a double call-out fee then."

"OK."

Hannah knew that made sense, but there was something about her dad's tone she couldn't read. She wasn't sure her dad had ever mentioned any sort of cost saving in front of her.

"I'll call him now and let him know he'll have another to see," Lucy said, seeming pleased to have something to do, and Hannah thanked her before heading back out. Glancing back, she frowned. She'd interrupted something, she just wasn't sure what.

"Hello, Hannah."

Hannah jumped down from the fence where she had been sitting, waiting for the vet's arrival.

Alistair smiled as he approached. "Your dad told me what you did. Buying a pony in Writley Park. Proper pony-book stuff!"

Alistair was wearing a checked shirt rolled up to his elbows. He had a calming presence that could soothe even the flightiest of ponies.

He listened to Bella's heart. "Hmm. Underweight, probably needs worming too, but nothing a bit of TLC can't fix." He paused. "How old did it say she was in her passport? Nine?"

"Yes," Hannah said, remembering how Rollo had told them the passport was likely false. "Nine."

Alistair shook his head. "Let me look at her teeth, but I reckon there's a few more years on top of that. And she's definitely had at least one foal."

"Oh, Bella." Hannah stroked the little mare's forehead. "You're safe now."

The grey pony stood quietly as Alistair looked into

her mouth with a head torch. "Ah," he said. "As I thought."

He clicked his head torch off and looked at Hannah. "I would say she's closer to her mid-teens. fifteen, sixteen perhaps. I imagine they put her through the sale as nine because it's the ideal age for a lot of buyers. Not too young, not too old."

"So her passport *is* fake, then?" Hannah said. "That's the age it said." She handed the document to Alistair to read.

"Yes, almost certainly." He clicked his torch back on and put the gag back into Bella's mouth so he could safely look at her teeth again.

"What I have noticed, though, is this tooth here. See?" Hannah looked, not really understanding what she was supposed to be looking at. Teeth always made her feel a bit squeamish. "It's an unusual presentation, where one of the teeth sticks out slightly. Won't cause her any problems, though. I remember a pony here a few years ago who had similar."

He removed the gag and gave Bella a pat. "I'm fairly sure that was a grey mare too," he said with a frown. "I might just check my files."

As Alistair got back into his car with a wave, Hannah

chewed on her thumbnail. Her mind was racing. Her dad thought he'd seen Bella before, but dismissed it, then there was the way the little mare had reacted to Ashley. And Ashley had very firmly put a stop to any filming. Now she knew Bella was at least six years older than she'd thought, and with Alistair's comment about her teeth it all seemed too much of a coincidence. Taking a deep breath, she headed towards her dad's office.

Henry Boland was at his desk, a coffee mug next to him as he tapped away on a keyboard. He hadn't seen Hannah approach, and she watched as he drummed his fingers on the polished wood and then stared out of the side window as if concentrating hard on something. As she knocked on the door, he looked up sharply before his features relaxed into a smile.

"Hannah," he said, quickly gathering some paperwork around him. "All OK? How's Bella? All OK with Alistair?"

"She's good," Hannah said. "Actually, Dad." She paused, tracing an "o" on the carpet with her dusty jodhpur boots. "Bella is who I wanted to talk about."

Was it her imagination or did her dad's expression change? She couldn't quite read it.

"Yes?"

"I just wondered," Hannah said, all in a rush, "you know you thought you recognised her when you first saw her? Do you think you might know her?"

"No," Henry said, his voice brisk. "I was mistaken. We did have a similar mare in a few years ago, but not the same one. I checked." He paused and then smiled widely. "Anyway," he said, chuckling, "it just shows how the years are going by. I worked out the mare we had in would be much older. And Bella's, what, eight, nine? Definitely not the same."

Hannah's stomach flipped. "Actually Alistair thought she might be older," she said. "Maybe mid-teens."

Henry looked up. "Really?" he said with a frown. "Well, sometimes these ponies, when they come over in a boat, details get mixed. Grey ponies do look similar. But I'm sure she's not the same pony."

It was as though he was talking to a much younger child. Hannah shook her head. "Alistair mentioned her teeth," she continued. "He thought—"

"She's not the same pony. I promise. I'll have a word with Alistair." He smiled.

Don't worry about it, Hannah. Just get on with it, Hannah.

She looked at him as he turned back to his screen, clearly dismissing her. Was he telling the truth? She wasn't sure. She wasn't sure about anything any more.

The long summer days seemed to blend into each other. It was hot from dusk to dawn, and aside from the odd ferocious rain shower, the sun continued to blaze down on Heartwood. Ponies were ridden either very early or very late, before being turned out for the night to enjoy some grazing without the flies bothering them. The film crew tried to get all their shots done in the morning, before the sun made everyone too hot and bothered for the job.

Now Bella had been vaccinated and wormed, Henry had allowed Hannah to turn her out with Delilah. Bella was the gentlest pony, and it broke Hannah's heart every time she thought about what her fate would have been had Rollo not stepped in to save her. Bella hadn't quite fully settled, but she was gaining weight and looking healthier. She was starting to recognise Hannah's footsteps in the morning and now whickered softly when she approached. Hannah solely looked after her, but she noticed Ashley kept well away from the grey mare anyway.

No more had been said about the similarities between her and the pony from years ago, and Alistair hadn't been in touch, or if he had, no one had told Hannah.

"Have you asked your dad again?" Gaby said as she leaned over the stable door one afternoon. "The vet was sure about her age, wasn't he?"

"I know," Hannah said. "No, I can't talk to my dad. He just closes up every time I mention anything about her past. As far as he's concerned, he had a pony similar to her, but not her. Without paperwork, or any history, how do I prove it?"

"Tricky." Gaby frowned. "If we knew something about her past, then we could help her. See if we could find out how she ended up at the sale. She must have such a story, and we don't know anything about her! I wish she could talk."

Hannah thought for a moment. "Millie's got so many followers online. I bet if she posted about Bella, someone would know something."

But when she ran over to Millie, untacking after filming on Gem, Millie just shrugged. "Why?"

"Because I thought it would be nice to show that we help ponies as well as all the shows and stuff," Hannah said. "And maybe we could find something out about Bella's past?"

"I don't know," Millie said doubtfully. "Yes, she's

super sweet, but she's your project. It doesn't exactly give the right impression of Heartwood, does it? We don't really *help* ponies. We're not a rescue centre…"

"She's not my project." Hannah scowled at her sister. "She's my pony. She's my friend."

"I know, and it's *so* nice," said Millie, "but maybe just keep her separate to … ummm … like, the other stuff we do here. What would Dad's clients think? We're an exclusive place. Not really set up for ponies like Bella. She's a one-off."

Hannah walked back to Bella and Gaby and placed her arms round Bella's grey neck. She wasn't as pure white as Hannah had initially thought. She had some black flecks through her coat like stars, which you could only see if you looked really closely. Hannah was starting to know every inch of her, from the pink snip between her nostrils to her white eyelashes. Bella was coming out of her shell with every day that passed and had the sweetest personality, gently affectionate and loving. She was starting to show a sense of humour too. Once Hannah had climbed over the pen hurdles and Bella had grabbed at the zip on her waistcoat, tugging it up and down. She no longer flinched away from being handled, and her eyes were starting to sparkle.

How could Millie say that? Hannah thought angrily. Bella was nothing to hide away or be ashamed of. She was a pony who deserved a home where she was safe. And from the personality that was starting to shine through there must have been someone, somewhere along the way, who had loved her once. Perhaps someone who was missing her, who wondered how her life had turned out. It would be so nice to reassure them she was safe. And suddenly Hannah had an idea. If no one was going to help her, she would do it on her own!

"Let me read it through," Gaby said.

Hannah passed her the phone, her heart racing. She'd logged into the account Millie had set up for her, and which Millie had begged her to use to "support the brand". Aside from two photos of Wolfie, there was nothing else there.

"*We came across Bella at Writley Park on the day of the festival,*" Gaby read aloud. "*It was like we were meant to be there. She'd been bought in a terrible state by a man who couldn't keep her, but he had saved her from a possible horrible fate. Since getting her home, she's starting to get back to full health, and she's the sweetest pony. We also found out she's most likely older than the age given, more like late teens. She has an unusual tooth, but that's all we know. We'd love to know about her history. If you recognise her, please send me a message. She didn't have a name. We called her Bella after Lulabella who we were supposed to see play, although we never got there. Thank you so much."*

Gaby nodded approvingly. "Sounds good. And you've tagged Millie and the official Boland yard account. That should get some views. I love the photo. Doesn't she look gorgeous?"

Hannah had asked Freddie to take a photo of Bella by the cherry tree. Although still underweight, she was a completely different pony to the one Vanessa had transported home, and with her ears pricked and a slight breeze lifting her white mane, and the fluffy cream head collar setting off her pretty face, she had taken Hannah's breath away.

"Look at these!" Freddie had said, showing Hannah the camera screen. "She's got something special about her; it's the eyes, I think."

Hannah had selected a photo of Bella side on. She'd been watching Delilah prance in the field and her ears were pricked fully forward.

"OK." Hannah took a deep breath, her thumb hovering over the post button. "Here goes!"

Chapter Ten

Clattering out of the yard on Wolfie and Buzz, Hannah and Gaby were in high spirits. Hannah felt giddy with exhilaration over what she had just done, and it was so good to ride with her best friend again. The girls headed on to the lane that led out towards the moors. Hannah had timed her post with Millie being tied up with Horsetalk, so she knew she wouldn't be able to check her phone for at least an hour. They needed time for the post to gather momentum, and Millie was sure to want to shut it down.

For a while they wound their way up through the gorse, climbing higher and higher, feeling the cool breeze on their warm skin. Hannah kept getting her phone out to check. People only followed her because of Millie. There were a number of likes and a few comments about how good it was to rescue a pony, but nothing that would help.

"See?" Gaby said as Hannah read one aloud. "It's not a bad thing. Everyone will think your yard is really kind."

There was no text or missed call from Millie, so Hannah knew she hadn't yet seen it. She felt a bit shaky; the initial adrenaline rush had gone.

Hannah and Gaby dismounted at the top of the hill and let Wolfie and Buzz graze as they shared some water and sweets. The shrill ring of Hannah's phone was like Millie's angry voice.

Hannah stared at her sister's name on the screen. "What should I do?"

"Ignore it," Gaby said airily. "Talk to her when you get back."

The missed call was swiftly followed by a text. Hannah imagined Millie jabbing at her phone.

"*I told you not to post anything!*" Hannah read the message aloud. "*She still looks awful. It's giving a really bad impression.*"

She looks awful because she was in an awful state! Hannah wrote back. *Why is it a problem?*

Heart beating hard, Hannah turned her phone off. At least they could enjoy the rest of the ride in peace.

As Hannah rode into the yard later, Wolfie on a loose rein, she felt her stomach tighten with apprehension. But to her surprise Millie wasn't waiting to shout at her.

"There's actually some really nice comments," she said. "Look at this. *Oh, Millie, that's amazing. She's lovely. Will you keep us updated?*" she read out loud, and smoothed back her flaxen hair. "I guess it is *quite* heart-warming."

While Millie was reading, Hannah rolled her eyes. Typical Millie; she didn't mind if it made her look good. But when Millie looked up, Hannah smiled at her. She needed Millie on her side.

"Thanks," she said. "And wouldn't it be nice to find out about Bella?"

"It would actually. She's really sweet. Just no more rescue missions, OK?"

"Deal." Hannah laughed, and for a few seconds it was like they were little again, giggling over things only they understood. But there was something else Hannah had to take care of.

"Can you not mention it to Mum and Dad for a couple of days?" she asked. Millie looked at her in surprise. "Just in case they want it deleted. I just want to see if anyone actually replies."

She didn't know what her mum and dad would think, but she didn't want them mentioning anything to Ashley.

Millie shrugged. "OK. You know Dad might do one of his spot checks, though. But he might be OK with it – this is *great* content! I am the social media queen!"

After a couple of hours, there were lots more comments, but still nothing useful about Bella's past. Millie was replying to them.

Thanks so much! Hannah read one of her comments to a particularly sweet message. *Yes, it's really rewarding. She's such a lovely pony, and now she's safe with us here at Heartwood.*

Hannah rolled her eyes again. But at least Millie was helping to spread the word about Bella, and maybe one of the responses would hold the key to the pony's past. Filling up hay nets in the barn, Hannah hummed to herself to keep her nerves at bay. Ashley walked past and didn't say anything, so she knew Millie had kept her side of the bargain. Now she just had to wait...

Hannah woke with a start. Outside her window the sky was an inky black and dotted with stars. She blinked, her head fuzzy. The chime of her phone notification rang in her ears. Her neon clock told her it was twelve thirty, so who on earth was messaging her now? Her first thought was Gaby or Jenson. What if they were in trouble? Blearily Hannah reached for her phone and read the screen, squinting as the glare cut through the dark.

I know your pony. The private message was a response to her post about Bella. *I looked after her. I'm so relieved she's safe.*

Hannah sat bolt upright, a surge of adrenaline coursing through her. She tapped to the profile of whoever had sent the message. It was set to private, but Hannah could just make out a photo of a pony in the profile picture. Hurriedly she typed back a message.

Hi! she wrote. *My grey pony? Bella? Is it her you know?*

Hannah stared at the screen for what felt an age,

and her head had begun to droop when another message flashed up.

She wasn't called Bella when I knew her. But it actually really suits her. Can we meet?

Hannah frowned. She knew about online safety and this didn't feel right at all, but before she could send a message declining, another text flashed up.

Sorry – I understand if you think I'm not real. My name's Cara. I can come to Varquis Show on Saturday. What about there? Before I messaged I saw your name on the start times online.

Varquis was a big date in the showjumping calendar, at one of the prestigious arenas on the coast, just outside Writley. Hannah and Millie were both competing there, and Hannah was due to meet the new owner of Wolfie. Horsetalk would be filming it all. There would be plenty of people about; it was a big public space. Hannah thought about it. Perhaps she could ask Gaby to meet her there for backup.

OK. Hannah took a deep breath as she typed back. *What time?*

Early? About eight. The answer came back immediately. *In the Nosebag Café?*

Hannah bit her lip, staring at her phone, her fingers hovering on the keys. This person, Cara, knew about the show and she knew about the Nosebag Café, the favourite café among competitors, though that was public knowledge. Did she *really* know Bella? Suddenly Hannah felt a bit foolish, thinking of all the school lessons about online safety. The start times at Varquis were in the public domain. Whoever was writing could be *anyone*. She felt a little bubble of panic. She had to try a test...

Before I agree, how can you prove that you know Bella?

She watched the icon on the screen whirr around, indicating that Cara was writing back – if indeed she was even a girl called Cara. Hannah felt her panic grow. The reply flashed back, and Hannah had to read it a couple of times to make sense of it.

She's got two perfect whorls under her mane. Hannah stared at her phone. *And on her offside knee, just on the inside, she's got a little pattern of grey hairs that look like a horseshoe. I used to call it her lucky mark. See you Saturday? I'm quite short, dark hair.*

Hannah took a deep breath. She knew the whorls were there; she'd spent ages grooming out Bella's silky mane. But she'd never noticed the mark on Bella's knee. Instead of replying, she pulled a wool jumper over her pyjamas and crept out of her bedroom, grabbing a torch from the dresser in the hall.

The air outside was cool. Across the clear sky a half-moon turned the surrounding moors silver. Hannah's footsteps rang so loudly across the quiet yard she felt almost like she was intruding on the peace of the night.

Reaching Bella's pen in the barn, she smiled as the little mare whickered. She was resting a leg and blinked sleepily as Hannah let herself in. Taking care not to shine the torch at the mare's face, she crouched and gently ran a hand down Bella's front leg, following her fingers with the light. There. She traced the outline of a smattering of grey flecks and took a sharp intake of breath. Just as Cara had described there was a small but strangely perfect horseshoe shape. Her hand shaking slightly, Hannah dug her phone out of her pyjama shorts pocket.

Saturday, she typed. *I'll be there.*

Hannah drummed her feet nervously on the lorry floor as the enormous vehicle pulled slowly through Varquis's big gates.

Millie looked at her. "Nervous?"

"A bit," Hannah said, because it was true – only she wasn't nervous about the jumping. Gaby nudged her arm from the other side, and the girls nodded at each other. Although Gaby's mum would be picking her up before Hannah's round started, Hannah was very glad to have her friend by her side. Even though Cara seemed to know Bella, and even though they were meeting in public, Hannah felt much safer knowing Gaby would be with her. She looked at Millie, who was engrossed in her phone again. Once she would have asked Millie to come with her, but everything seemed different now.

"All right then," Millie said as Henry Boland manoeuvred into a parking spot and Gem gave a shrill whinny from the back. She pulled out a compact mirror from a little bag and smoothed her ponytail before smiling at her reflection. "Let's go!"

"Gaby and I are going for a hot chocolate," Hannah said, glancing at her friend. "If that's OK?"

"That sounds nice," Henry said. "The Nosebag is still the best show café around. Just make sure you leave enough warm-up time. Are you meeting any of your friends today, Millie?"

Hannah saw a shadow flit across her sister's face.

"Oh, not today," she said brightly. "Too busy. I've got a meet and greet."

Hannah watched as Millie skipped off, flanked by the film crew, who were already waiting for them. She couldn't remember the last time Millie met up with any friends.

After checking on Wolfie and Gem, who were happily munching hay, Hannah and Gaby hurried across to the big café on the other side of the show centre. Millie was just outside the main arena, where there was already a queue of people waiting to meet her, mainly excited girls clutching things for her to sign.

Heading inside the café, Hannah looked around, her heart pounding. Gaby nudged her, and Hannah followed her gaze.

"Is that her?"

There was one girl sitting on her own. Most other people wore smart clothes, white breeches if they were competing. The girl at the table in front of them was small and slight in a baggy grey sweatshirt with patches sewn on to her jean shorts. Her dark hair was thrown up into a high ponytail and she tapped nervously on the table with nails hidden under chipped black polish. As she looked up, she met Hannah's gaze and moved her lips into a tight half-smile.

"Cara," Hannah muttered. Her mouth dry, she waved shyly and walked over. Finally she'd find out a little more about the pony who had captured her heart! Taking a deep breath, she smiled. "I'm Hannah Boland. This is Gaby, my friend," she added, as Gaby took a seat.

The girl's face relaxed. "Hi, I'm Cara."

Hannah guessed Cara was older than her, but not by much, She had a quick, nervous manner about her and talked very fast. She produced an envelope of photos from her rucksack, spreading them out on the table so Hannah could see them. The pony in the pictures was unmistakably Bella but in better health.

"She was called Fifty," Cara said. "Because that's what she cost. Bella suits her so much better. Fifty was a horrible name."

"That's her!" Hannah gazed in wonder at one photo, showing it to Gaby, who was wide-eyed.

"That's definitely her," Gaby agreed. She looked at Cara, and back to the photo. In it, the little mare was tied up to a wooden stable, which was half covered by a tarpaulin. There was a rusty car parked up next to the stable and a couple of dogs lying down beside it.

"This was when she was at Justine's," Cara explained. "I worked for Justine for years."

"For years?" Hannah asked. "How old *are* you?"

"I'm sixteen," Cara said with a wry smile. "I know, I'm tiny. But I've been working there since I was small. It was somewhere to escape to. I loved the ponies. And I used to think the world of Justine."

Hannah blinked. "Who *is* Justine?" she asked.

A look of pain flashed across Cara's pale face. "Justine was my boss," she said. "But she was like family. She took me in when my parents –" She paused. "Let's just say they weren't around. I was so grateful to her. And at first I loved it. Ponies to ride and my own bedroom if I needed a space to stay, even if it was in a caravan. At first it was just occasionally, then Justine's yard became my home. The ponies saved me."

"So what happened?" Hannah asked. "And where does Bella fit in?"

Cara took a deep breath. "I wasn't comfortable with a lot of the things Justine did," she said. "But it took me a while to see it. At first I was just so grateful to have somewhere to stay, and then I thought I needed to stay loyal. It took me ages to realise Justine didn't care about me at all. I was just cheap labour for her. I heard her boasting about it to her friend. How she didn't need to pay a groom because she had me, and I cost nothing to keep. They were laughing at me, mocking me. And after that…"

"Go on," Hannah said gently.

"I started to see it all for what it was," Cara said, briefly closing her eyes. "Justine bought ponies in, then sold them on for a massive profit, or bred from the mares when she could."

"So buying and producing?" Gaby asked, looking at Hannah, and Hannah knew what she was thinking: it sounded pretty similar to what her own family did.

"Exactly. But Justine didn't care where they went or what she did to get the money," Cara continued. "I saw ponies who reared over backwards go on to be sold as safe children's ponies, and one who had a serious tendon injury put on loads of painkillers and sold as a top jumper. I had to tell so many lies, but I was so worried about losing the only home I knew, I kept doing it. I hate myself for it, but I didn't think I had a choice. When the new owners complained she got really nasty – threatening, all sorts. No one dared cross her or sue her. She got away with it all. She's *still* getting away with it. She's untouchable."

"And what about Bella ... I mean Fifty?" Hannah asked.

Cara's face softened. "She was special," she said. "She was the most beautiful pony we'd ever had at Justine's. But for some reason she had lost her nerve jumping. Justine knew the man who was selling her and knew her heritage was good, so decided to breed from her instead of selling her straight on. They had some sort of deal going on, her and this man. She got Bella cheap, but they were going to split any profits from breeding her.

"After a while, Bella had a colt. But it didn't go to plan." She shook her head, looking upset. "He was such a weak little thing. He needed extra bottle feeding. Fifty – sorry – Bella got really sick and couldn't produce enough milk, and Justine wouldn't pay the vet bills or bother bottle feeding. Because she paid next to nothing for her, she would have just let them both die.

"But I stayed up all night for weeks, making sure he survived. Justine told me I could have the foal, that he was worthless. Bella recovered but she couldn't have another baby. They tried again, but…" She dropped her head. "This time the foal didn't make it. And Bella had done her time for Justine by then. She had no use for her, and Bella was so weak after that, so she sold her on really quickly. I don't know who bought her, but she obviously ended up in the auction."

Hannah was completely transfixed. "What happened to the foal you saved?"

"I called him Dusty. He's nearly four now." Cara's voice cracked. "She took him, one day when I was out. Just disappeared. She won't tell me where he is, but I *know* he's not sold yet. That tiny little foal she called worthless – he was my reason for everything." She wiped a tear away. "I'm so worried about him. He'll be so scared without me. I wish I knew where he was. He's mine. I have the paperwork to prove it, but it's at Justine's."

"Oh, Cara," Hannah said, feeling helpless. "Do you still work for Justine now?"

Cara shook her head. "No," she said. "After what happened with Bella and Dusty, I'd finally had enough. I started building up evidence of what she was doing to report her somehow. But I think she must have suspected me and she threw me out the day after Dusty disappeared. I'm OK, though," she said quietly. "I actually work quite locally to you. A boarding kennels. It's nice."

Hannah thought about Heartwood, about her enormous bedroom and the warm kitchen full of food. Despite how she felt about her parents and Millie at the moment, she had a family, and a home. Cara was younger than her sister and had nothing.

Suddenly Gaby nudged her and looked at the

clock on the wall. "Oh, I have to go," Hannah said regretfully. "I need to be on Wolfie. Will you keep in touch? You can come and see Bella any time. I really hope you find Dusty."

Cara nodded. "Thank you," she said, looking very young hunched up in her chair.

Then Hannah had a thought. "Do you happen to know which yard Bella came from?" she said. "I wonder if we could trace them, find out more about her. Perhaps then you could find Dusty?"

But Cara shook her head. "Justine always kept things like that on the downlow," she said. "I remember a man dropping her off. He was really arrogant. He came a few times while I was there, with different ponies, but Bella was the one I remember most. I've no idea where the man was from, though. Justine got ponies from this posh yard sometimes, when they didn't want to sell them themselves. Could have been there?"

Hannah's blood ran cold. It couldn't be, could it? Of all the people, all the yards in the country, it surely couldn't be? Even though she'd had her suspicions, it was as though someone had poured icy water on her.

"Cara," she asked slowly, "you don't have any more recent photos of Justine's yard, do you?"

Cara shrugged. "Sure," she said, getting her phone out. "Justine had it all cleaned up in the last couple of years. She liked flash things, designer clothes and stuff, and I guess she thought a posher yard made her look more respectable. It was just a front, though. She was still the same underneath."

Tapping at the screen, Cara turned it round so Hannah could see, and instantly she knew. Blue doors; those fields. It was the same place Ashley had photographed when he'd sold sweet Tolly.

All the little things that had been niggling Hannah for a while finally added up. The mistreated mare had known where she was the day Hannah had unloaded her at Heartwood. Bella hadn't just come to Heartwood; she had *returned* to Heartwood.

Chapter Eleven

Head reeling, Hannah quickly exchanged numbers with Cara. They were forever connected now by Hannah's beautiful pony Bella and her lost foal who held Cara's heart. But something had stopped her from telling Cara she knew the truth. She had to be completely sure first. She ran to get Wolfie ready and bumped straight into Millie outside the café.

"Hannah, whoa!"

Millie was in good mood, as she always

was after meeting her fans. "Don't you need to be on Wolfie?" Millie checked the diamond watch on her wrist. "Now?"

"Yep," Hannah muttered, unable to look at her sister.

Gaby gave Millie an icy look. "She's heading there now," she said, and Millie held her hands up before walking off.

"All right, all right," she said. "I only asked."

She sounded as perky as ever. Did *Millie* know about Bella? Hannah remembered the way Millie and her dad had told the Horsetalk reporters about their business, how each pony ended up in the perfect home, how the greatest care was taken. And yet Bella had been sold to a horrible woman and then discarded like rubbish when the breeding hadn't gone to plan. Surely Millie didn't know. It went against everything her wholesome brand stood for. But there *was* another world out there. It had been there all along. And they were part of it.

"Come on, Han," her dad said cheerfully. He was holding Wolfie, who was already tacked up. "Think you lost track of time in the Nosebag."

Hannah could barely look at him. Instead, she gave Wolfie a pat, fastened the chinstrap on her hat and swung herself into the saddle. She just needed to be on the pony she loved.

Somehow Hannah managed a clear first round, which she knew was all down to sweet Wolfie. She was merely a passenger. She could tell by Millie's raised eyebrow that she knew something was up as she headed out of the ring.

"You looked as though you weren't thinking at all," Millie said crossly. "Good thing Wolfie knew what he was doing. Try to at least look professional," she added with a hiss, gesturing over to where Logan was standing with his camera. "It's being recorded. And his new owner is watching."

"At least you know who she is," Hannah muttered under her breath, but Millie must have heard her.

She swung round. "What do you mean by that?" she asked, but Hannah wasn't prepared to broach the subject. Not yet.

"Nothing. I'm just hot."

Hannah headed over to the shade of a tree overlooking the warm-up arena to wait for her jump-off. As she dismounted, suddenly her legs gave way and she slid down, kneeling on the floor as Wolfie lowered his sleek head down to her.

"Thank you." She rested her head against his,

grateful for his solid form. Shutting her eyes, she thought about what she had learned just an hour or so ago. It hadn't sunk in yet.

"That was amazing."

A voice made Hannah jump. Looking up, she saw a young girl approach. She seemed familiar – then Hannah twigged. She'd seen her on the yard in immaculate breeches, hopping out of a shiny four-by-four. Wolfie's new owner. What was her name? Hannah racked her brains. Erin! That was it.

"Thanks," Hannah mumbled. "He's an amazing pony."

Erin sighed, patting Wolfie's neck. "I know. I can't wait until I can do all that too."

Hannah felt a pang of guilt, realising that Wolfie's new owner seemed really nice. She'd agreed to the Horsetalk documentary because it would mean a few more weeks with Wolfie, and yet his new owner was having to wait and put her own summer on hold. She'd never given much thought to the owners before, only thinking about her own upset when the ponies she had bonded with were sent off to their new homes. But seeing Erin, who was still patting Wolfie, gently talking to him and smoothing his black mane, she realised how reassuring it was to know he had such a lovely owner to go to. That's what she had thought always happened, what she had been led to believe. But not for Bella. She shook her head, her thoughts darkening.

"He needs warming up again," Hannah said. "Would you like to ride him?"

Erin smiled, her eyes sparkling. "Yes, please!" Then she bit her lip. "Would that be OK? Am I allowed?"

"Of course you're allowed," Hannah said. "He's your pony!"

Her dad probably wouldn't approve, but Hannah didn't much care what Dad or Millie thought at the moment. All she saw in front of her was a girl desperate to ride her pony. Handing over her hat, she smiled as Erin fastened it on her head and hopped up into the saddle, throwing her arms round Wolfie's neck as she did so. Soon Erin was trotting round the warm-up arena, in perfect sync with Wolfie. She was a lovely quiet rider. Hannah winced as she thought about the contrast to Bella's journey. Both ponies had started in the same yard, yet couldn't be more different.

Hannah's mind wasn't on the competition at all. As she cantered round the arena, all she could think about was Bella. How could she have been discarded like that?

Nudging Wolfie on, she was aware of Millie watching her, willing her to do well. Over the first, then the second, Wolfie's easy way of jumping relaxed her. But wait – there was a turn she was supposed to have made, wasn't there? Swinging him round too late, Wolfie was on the wrong stride. He caught the top pole of the spread with a clatter and sent it tumbling to the ground as the crowd groaned. It was an expensive mistake that would put them out of the top placings. Hannah winced as she carried on, making sure she didn't meet Millie's eye.

As they finished, Hannah gave the sweet bay pony a hug. It hadn't been his fault – it was all on her.

Millie had a brilliant second round, but as they loaded up both ponies and set up their hay nets, the atmosphere in the horsebox felt very frosty.

"What was up with you?" Henry Boland flicked on his indicators as he eased the big lorry out of the showground gates.

Hannah stared down at her boots. It was the first thing he'd said to her since the fault.

"Nothing," she muttered. "It just happened."

Millie folded her arms. "You've been in a weird mood all day," she said. "And that was such a stupid mistake." She ran her fingers through her ponytail and let out a short sigh. "But let's try and put a positive spin on it. It builds up the tension, doesn't it, before the championships? Showing the ups and downs of horses." She smiled at Hannah, who stared straight ahead.

"That's fine," Henry said shortly. "But it still wasn't great. Wolfie's owner paid a lot of money for him, and it wasn't exactly the best advert for us, was it?"

Hannah thought about Erin and the relief of knowing that Wolfie's new owner was a nice person. Then she thought about Cara. "*Bella* isn't the best advert for us," she muttered, and her dad turned to her, his expression incredulous.

Millie looked confused. "Bella?"

"Yes," Hannah said, the word almost a shout as she stopped trying to hold it in. "She was here before at Heartwood. But because she wasn't good enough, she got chucked out. She was sold to an awful dealer who tried to breed from her. You *did* recognise her."

Millie stared at her, her mouth agape.

Henry slammed his hand down on to the steering wheel. "What on earth are you talking about?!" he exploded. "That mare is not the same one I sold! I don't know what's got into you, Hannah, spinning this fantasy!"

"So *where* did she go? The mare you sold?" Hannah folded her arms, not giving in.

Her dad shook his head. "A home in the New Forest, a lady who wanted a companion pony," he said. "She went to a perfectly nice home!"

"Did Ashley tell you that?" Hannah continued, and Henry glanced at her. "And you believed him?"

"Of course I did. He had all the paperwork," Henry said crossly. "I know you and Ashley clash, Hannah, but he was born at Heartwood. Johno and he are family. He's always done right by me! I'd never let a pony go off to a bad dealer, *any* pony. Sometimes the ponies don't make the grade, but that doesn't mean they go to awful places. I insist on that! And for the last time, Hannah, that pony of yours is completely new here. I'm not having this conversation any more!"

Hannah glanced at her sister. She was almost certain now that Millie knew nothing. She knew by the way Millie was looking at her that she was totally confused. She couldn't tell if her dad knew the truth or if he was just in denial, but she also knew he wasn't going to help her uncover Bella's past. This was something she'd have to do on her own.

Finally a day came when Ashley had the afternoon off, Millie was filming with Horsetalk in Writley, and Mum and Dad had an appointment with the bank. At two p.m., dressed smartly, her mum kissed her goodbye. Hannah noticed she seemed on edge.

"We'll be a couple of hours," Lucy said. "At least."

Hannah waved them goodbye at the gate.

Perfect. Hannah ran across the yard and punched in the code for her dad's office. It wasn't out of bounds – she and Millie used to race his office chairs across the carpet when they were younger – but there had never been a reason to go snooping. She wasn't even sure what she was looking for. She opened one filing cabinet after another. *It's not like there will be a big file labelled "Dodgy Dealings",* she thought in frustration. She wanted solid proof that Bella had once lived on the yard. She remembered Cara's words, how "Fifty" had been sold from a good yard because she'd lost her nerve for some reason. And then she thought of sweet Tolly, who just didn't want to jump and had quickly been sold. She felt sick. Tolly was yet another discarded pony, a not-good-enough-to-be-a-Boland pony. How many more were there?

Hannah went through every hanging file in the cabinets but found nothing. *It's not as if he'd keep a photo of her*, she thought sadly. How could she prove Ashley was the one who'd dropped her off? He'd only deny it. There might be things on her dad's computer, but she had no way of getting access. She'd have to think of another way.

Later on, Hannah leaned over the fence watching Bella graze side by side with Delilah out in the little paddock, their shadows long in the evening sunshine.

"I know that mare. I said to Ashley, I know that pony, but he said I was imagining it. But I do. I know her."

It was Johno, over to visit his son. He'd walked up behind her and now leaned against the fence next to her. His gaze was fixed on Bella, recognition lighting up his face.

"Can't remember what I did this morning –" he gave Hannah a rueful smile – "but I know that pony." He clicked his fingers so Bella walked over to him. She wasn't wary of Johno, who'd always had a gentle way about him.

Hannah gasped. "Do you, Johno? What do you know?"

Johno furrowed his forehead, the lines on his brow deep and sharply etched. "She was a grand little mare, came over from Ireland, in a boatload your father bought. But she was nervy. Talented – could have jumped the moon. Funny tooth, as I recall. But…" His face dropped, as if remembering something painful. "He never got it quite right. I told him. You can't rush a mare like that. I didn't see her after that. Hacking home she'd gone to, so I was told."

"What didn't get it right? Who?" Hannah asked desperately. "What happened?"

"I'm sorry, Hannah. I can't remember." Johno shook his head, looking upset. "I wish I could."

"It's OK, Johno."

Hannah gave him a hug. She knew he found it hard. But her mind was already in overdrive. Johno had known Bella here at Heartwood, and that was proof enough. And it sounded like something had gone very wrong…

Chapter Twelve

The thirtieth of August, the date of the showjumping championships, was looming, no longer just a faraway day in the future. Hannah and Cara were in regular contact, but they were no closer to finding Dusty. The hot sultry days of high summer were baking the ground hard.

Despite all the worry, this morning Hannah was going to do something she'd been looking forward to ever since Bella had first walked down the ramp at

Heartwood. The little mare was looking great, and Hannah knew it was time. She was going to ride her pony.

Hannah hummed happily to herself as she carefully placed the bridle over Bella's white ears. Bella's ears were surprisingly large. She remembered how Johno had once told her it was a sign of an honest pony. A stable space had finally become free, so Bella had recently moved out of her temporary pen in the barn and into a proper stable. Hannah was hopeful that it meant her parents had accepted her now, even if the tension around her past remained. Vanessa and Gaby leaned against the door as Hannah smoothed down the turquoise saddle pad, swiped from Millie's never-ending supply. It looked gorgeous on Bella, and Hannah smiled as the little mare danced a bit at the stable door, her eyes bright.

"She looks super, but be careful," Vanessa said. "Remember we don't know what she'll be like."

But Hannah trusted her instincts. So many times recently, as she'd walked Bella around the meandering lanes and the lower parts of the moors, she had been tempted to jump up on to her back. She would never rush Bella, but she felt sure she was ready. Placing a foot in the stirrup, she gave Bella a reassuring stroke and swung herself into the saddle as lightly as possible, gathering up the plaited reins of the bridle. The reins had once been Wispa's, and Hannah felt a huge mix of emotions at holding them again. Bella was her heart horse, the pony she'd been looking for, and so it was only right she had them. She nudged her on gently and the little mare responded joyfully. She didn't just walk; she floated. But as they reached the arena gate, Hannah felt Bella tense up and start to back off. Her ears went back, and she snorted.

Hannah shook her head, annoyed at herself for not thinking. "Of course. This is where it all went wrong before, isn't it? Don't worry, girl," she said, gesturing to Gaby and Vanessa to follow her. "I know the perfect place."

Opening the gate to the walkway round the fields, Hannah felt Bella instantly relax, her lovely ears pricked forward once again. A few of the ponies in the fields watched them, and Delilah gave a whinny. Heading round the path, under the cool of the overhanging willows, Hannah rode right to the boundary of their pony paddocks, crossing over a stream and laughing as Bella pawed enthusiastically at the water, then into a meadow that had recently been cut for hay.

"Trot her on," Vanessa said with a smile, walking beside her. "She looks absolutely lovely!"

So Hannah nudged her on, just the gentlest of touches, and Bella responded eagerly, springing into the most beautiful trot. They circled the meadow, and Bella could have been floating on air. She was so light, so soft and supple, her neck arched but not tense. Hannah couldn't help but laugh out loud. It was the best feeling ever.

Gaby was grinning from ear to ear, but Vanessa looked quite emotional.

"Been quite a while since I've seen a pony move like that," she said. "She's something very special, Hannah."

Hannah leaned forward and hugged Bella tightly. She wouldn't have minded if Bella was a poor mover. She was Hannah's pony through and through. But the fact she was starting to shine felt like a big one-up on whoever had sent her to the sale, and on Justine, who'd rejected the sweet mare when she couldn't make her any money, and on her dad and Ashley, who'd callously sold her in the first place. They'd started the awful chain of events. That first domino had been knocked over here at Heartwood.

"You know," Vanessa said thoughtfully, "I know

she's supposed to have lost confidence over fences, and certainly I'd leave it a while before I even attempted a cross pole, but perhaps it's just a case of her not having the right rider. There's something about you two." She smiled. "I have a good feeling."

Cara was waiting in the yard when Hannah returned, having said goodbye to Gaby and Vanessa. Bella gave Cara a whicker of recognition, and Cara laughed and stroked her nose.

"She looks so happy," she said. "I saw you when I cycled up the lane, trotting in the field. She's got an amazing trot. I always thought Dusty had the same trot too." She paused. "I hope you don't mind that I came for a quick visit."

Hannah jumped off and ran her stirrups up, giving Bella a pat. "That's all right! Have you got any further with tracking Dusty down?" she asked. She felt a pang of guilt, as she always did when she asked Cara about Dusty. She hoped Cara didn't suspect anything about where Bella originally came from. Hannah *knew* she'd think less of her if she did, and she wanted to put things right before she told her the awful truth. It was a fine balance between normal chit-chat and trying not to let slip what she'd found out.

Cara shook her head. "No," she said. "And I'd be stuck anyway without the paperwork. I wish I hadn't left it behind! Not that I was given any choice," she added miserably.

Hannah could feel her brain whirring into action, the bones of a plan starting to take shape. If she could get hold of the paperwork, that would put right some of what had gone on before.

"Cara," she said slowly, "do you have any idea where the paperwork might be?"

"I can picture exactly where," Cara said. "Why?"

"Well," Hannah said. "If you can't go back, can I go instead?" She knew exactly what it was she wanted to do, but she would need her friends' help again.

Later that evening, Hannah slipped off to her room, tapped the number that Cara had given her into her phone and held her breath as it rang.

"Hello?" The reply was brisk, almost unfriendly.

Hannah felt her stomach turn over. "Oh. Hi," she mumbled. "I ... I saw your advert on the internet and I wondered –" she cleared her throat – "I wondered if I could arrange a viewing?"

"Which one?" Justine – it had to be – snapped. "I've got several for sale."

"Oh!" Hannah bit her thumbnail, certain she'd blown it. "Um, the chestnut mare. The ten-year-old."

She held her breath, expecting Justine to hang up. She knew how young she sounded on the phone, and she'd fumbled her reply. But Justine sounded as though she was flicking through a calendar.

"Ten on Saturday," she said. "And don't be late; I won't wait for you."

Uttering a sigh of relief, Hannah thanked her and ended the call, her hands clammy. This would be scarier than she'd thought!

"Are you sure this is a good idea?"

Jenson twisted his hands together nervously, and Hannah could feel his leg drumming the floor of the bus. She took a deep breath, trying to stop her own nerves spilling over. She looked again at the directions Cara had scrawled on a piece of paper for her, along with a small silver key to the caravan. Even with Gaby and Jenson promising to work as a team with Hannah, Cara had been nervous about the plan, but Hannah had insisted.

"It's got to work," said Hannah. "Hopefully Justine hasn't thought to check the caravan yet. Cara said she never visited it when she lived there."

In the small bedside drawer, in an envelope with Cara's name on it, Hannah thought to herself for the millionth time. Proof that Dusty belonged to Cara. Justine had threatened to set the dogs on Cara if she set foot in the yard again. Hannah swallowed hard. What if they'd bitten off more than they could chew? They'd told everyone they had gone into Writley. No one *actually* knew where they were.

"How do I look?" Gaby smoothed her black hair. She'd put some make-up on to try to look older and Jenson had even brushed his hair. Hannah had found him some old clothes of Ashley's waiting to go to a charity shop, some breeches with a small darn and a freebie polo shirt, and Gaby was wearing some of her own riding clothes.

"Great," Hannah said, hoping her voice didn't sound too wobbly. "So, remember. You're hoping to buy a pony. And Jenson's your groom."

"Ha, not likely, Gabs," Jenson joked, but his smile didn't quite reach his eyes. He looked terrified and Hannah wished she could take his place. But there was no way she could be the one who saw Tolly. Hannah could easily be recognised from Millie's videos, and she knew the sweet chestnut mare would recognise her. Her heart hurt at the thought of Tolly standing there, and not being able to run and hug her. But she had a job to do.

After a ten-minute walk from the nearest bus stop, Hannah stopped at a five-bar wooden gate with a horseshoe on it. From the road it looked a pleasant enough place. Hannah looked at the sign and then at the note in her pocket.

"This is it."

"OK, then." Gaby took a deep breath and she and Jenson walked through the gate, leaving Hannah to follow Cara's directions to the back path. From where she was standing she could just see the yard, and there was Tolly. Sweet, kind Tolly. Hannah watched Justine welcome Gaby and Jenson. Jenson was nodding, and Justine was gesticulating. She was tall and lean and had a baseball cap over a long bleach-blonde ponytail.

"How old *are* you?" Hannah could hear snatches of conversation, and recognised the same clipped, snappy tone from the phone. Justine's face seemed to match her voice – sharp and cold, her heavily made-up eyes narrowed against a tanned face.

Was it her imagination, or did Gaby shoot her a panicked look? They weren't tacking Tolly up. In fact, they were now starting to back away. Jenson was saying something now, his hands up. He looked scared. Hannah had to act fast. Sneaking through the gap, she crept round to the caravan, her breathing ragged with fear. Her hands fumbling, she managed to turn the key in the lock. Looking around, her gaze fell on a small bedside table. Hannah opened the drawer, and there, underneath an old copy of *Horse & Hound*, was an envelope. Hannah grabbed it and, after a second's pause, also took the only thing on the top of the bedside table: a small framed photograph of a foal. She sneaked back out and locked the door, and then gave a start of horror as she noticed Tolly still tied up in the yard, but Gaby and Jenson nowhere to be seen. Her heart crashing against her ribs, she ran back to the gate. She could hear dogs barking, and any second now she was sure Justine would step into her path. Pushing the gate, she ran as fast as she could back to the road, where she met Jenson and Gaby, who were both pale-faced.

"You made it!" Gaby clung to Hannah's arm. "We never got as far as riding."

"Only just!" Hannah took a deep breath, trying to steady her breathing. Her legs were weak, her hands shaking, but she was clutching the envelope. She could still see hear the dogs barking, and wanted to laugh hysterically, half out of fear, half out of sheer disbelief that she'd actually got Cara's papers. She'd never done anything like this in her life!

"Let's get out of here," Gaby said. "Quickly."

But just as they were about to cross the road and head back to the bus stop, a car pulled up and a pleasant-looking woman hopped out. She looked at her phone, and then at the gate and frowned.

Hannah couldn't help it. She had to say something. Before either of her friends could stop her, she ran over. "E-excuse me," she stammered. The woman turned to her with a look of surprise. "Are you going to look at the chestnut pony?"

"I am. Why?" The woman sounded confused, but not unkind. "I'm a bit early."

"Please," Hannah said, "if you buy her, can you let me know? I just want to know she's OK."

Digging in her pocket, she found a biro and an old leaflet from one of the shows and scrawled her number on it. "There," she said. "Please. It's a long story."

"OK." The woman looked doubtful but took the piece of leaflet. "But I have to say, I probably won't. My friend warned me about buying from a dealer, but I'd already made the appointment. I thought I'd just come along to look." She paused and shook her head. "But, like I said, it's probably a no."

She looked up as the dogs' barking grew louder, and Gaby grabbed Hannah's arm.

"Han," she said urgently. "The bus!"

They ran. They'd got what they needed. Hannah just had to hope Tolly would be OK.

"That was scary." Gaby shook her head. They were safely on the bus now, heading back to Heartwood, and Hannah was only just starting to calm down. "She sussed us out straight away."

"She knew I wasn't a groom!" Jenson said. "Said she had no time for joyriders. What does *that* mean?"

Hannah nodded. "Like, people who turn up for a free pony ride with no intention of actually buying." She'd heard Ashley complain about it in the past. "She probably thought you were just kids."

"Well," Gaby said, a small smile on her face, "we are. Still, we got what we needed."

Hannah couldn't stop thinking about sweet Tolly still in the yard. They couldn't just steal her back. As much as it pained her to admit it, Tolly had been sold. By *her* own family.

"What was she like?" Hannah asked curiously. "Justine?"

Gaby frowned. "Nice when we got there, but

then really not. She was, like, *hard*," she said with a shudder. "She just had this vibe. I wouldn't want to be on the wrong side of her."

"We nearly were!" Jenson said. "Imagine if we'd got caught." He gestured at the envelope Hannah was still clutching. "So what happens next?"

"Honestly," said Hannah, "I'm not sure."

Chapter Thirteen

The evening sun stretched lazily across the pale sand, sending out a long shadow of Hannah and Wolfie as they trotted round the school. Hannah half closed her eyes, enjoying the warm air, the golden rays bouncing off the conker brown of Wolfie's coat. The ping of her phone jolted her awake. It was the message she'd been waiting for since she got back from Justine's early that afternoon. Cara was on her way over.

Hannah had just finished making up Wolfie's bed for the night when Cara cycled into the yard. Luckily Ashley had finished for the evening and was in his cottage, probably in front of the TV. He'd come out much later for night checks. Her mum and dad were in the house. Millie was in the yard, but Hannah thought on her feet.

"Millie, this is Cara," she said. "She, er, she goes to my school. She's new."

"Oh, hi," Millie said unenthusiastically and sidled away.

Hannah sighed with relief, grateful for Millie's lack of interest in any of her friends.

Now, in the sanctuary of Wolfie's stable, Hannah passed Cara the envelope and the photo.

"Thank you!" Cara clutched them to her chest, then opened the envelope. "See, it's here. His rightful passport, and the letter Justine wrote, signing him over to me."

She touched the glass of the frame, gazing at the photo. "He's changed loads since this was taken," she added sadly. "He's all grown up now, and his colour's changing, he's greying out."

"If Justine still has him, would she be able to sell him without these documents?" asked Hannah.

"She knows the right people," Cara explained. "She'll just have false papers made."

"Like Bella's," Hannah said. "I can't believe I never knew this world existed. Now that you can prove Dusty is yours, can you go to the police?"

Cara gazed at her in a level sort of way. "It's my word against hers," she said. "Justine knows people. Who's going to believe someone like me?" She seemed to Hannah to look suddenly smaller and younger. "I just want Dusty back. And now I can try and find him. Thank you, Hannah. I owe you so much."

But Hannah frowned. "You can't do it on your own," she said. "Let us help you."

Cara shook her head. "No," she said. "It's amazing you found Bella, and that led you to me, but honestly it's OK. You've got your own life; you don't need to get mixed up in mine."

Hannah gave Wolfie a pat, a surge of guilt coursing through her. She had to tell Cara the truth, however hard. She couldn't put it off any longer.

"I already am," she said, and she took a deep breath. "There's something I need to tell you."

Hannah got them cans of lemonade from the tack-room fridge and the girls sat round the table while Hannah told Cara what she'd found out, from her discovery of Bella, to the way Ashley wouldn't let her appear in the documentary, Alistair the vet's comment, Johno's observation and finally Tolly.

"You're telling me you didn't know any of this when you found Bella?" asked Cara incredulously.

Hannah shook her head. "No," she said. "But now I think about it, I wonder if I was so drawn to Bella because I knew her when I was younger. Maybe I remembered her without realising."

Hannah had a memory of when she was little: Millie riding a pony, while Hannah was lifted on to a Shetland. Bella would have been in the yard when Hannah had just started school. Perhaps Hannah had patted her, given her a brush with the pink grooming kit she'd got for Christmas.

"So the guy who dropped Tolly off," Cara said, "does he still work here?"

"Yes," Hannah said miserably. "Ashley. He's treated like a member of the family. Everyone trusts him."

More than me sometimes, she thought.

"So are your mum and dad aware of what goes on?" Cara asked with a frown. "Do they know where the ponies are sold?"

"That's the thing," Hannah said. "I don't know. Dad's always made a big deal about placing ponies in the right homes, and he loves his horses." She thought about Mistral and Delilah, and how soppy her dad was over them. "But then he can be really ruthless about selling ponies on quickly to make space for the next potential star. I just don't understand."

"I guess he just trusts Ashley to do the right thing then. Simple as that?"

Hannah looked at her feet. She hoped her dad was totally unaware. Or was it that he turned a blind eye, knowing Ashley wasn't doing things the "Boland yard way", but preferring to stay ignorant of the details? That would make him almost as bad as Ashley.

"I guess," she said. "Ashley must tell him that he sells the ponies to a good home, and then sells them instead to people like Justine." She took a deep breath. "Dad's probably just relieved not to have the problem any more, so doesn't question it."

"And Justine offered the right arrangement," Cara said slowly. "There's always money involved with Justine. Something that suited her and Ashley. They're both out for everything they can get."

"Do you hate me?" Hannah whispered, but Cara looked at her in amazement.

"No!" she said. "Why would you say that?"

"All this, my family, the yard." She watched as a

sweet pony called Oscar fiddled with a head collar hanging outside his stable. "I promise I didn't know. But now I do I'm trying to put it right."

"Hannah, I don't hate you," Cara said, smiling. "I knew you were a good person the minute I met you! Besides, if Bella likes you, I do too."

Hannah smiled back gratefully. Telling Cara the truth had taken a weight off her shoulders.

Cara took a breath. "Better get off," she said, and went to pick up her bike.

"Do you still work at the boarding kennels?"

"Yep," Cara said. "And they've got accommodation. But it can't be forever; they're retiring soon. I'd love to work with horses but Justine would never give me a reference and people can be quite, um…" She bit her lip. "They just look at me and my background and how young I am and they don't trust me… And there's Justine, always invited to sit in a posh box at Olympia."

It reminded Hannah of Rollo at the festival, talking about being judged. And yet he'd saved Bella.

"But the kennels are OK." Cara smiled. "I like the dogs. The owners are kind. I'll find something else when I have to. I always do."

"Please come over whenever you like," Hannah

said, and Cara reached over and gave her a hug.

"Thanks," she said. "I'd like that. It's so nice to see Bella again."

But she looked wistful, and Hannah knew she was thinking about Dusty.

Later on, Hannah sat on Bella's hay manger, watching the grey mare eat. She couldn't imagine life without her now. Wispa had been very special, but Bella was truly hers. Hannah had never believed in fate, but what else could explain her coming across Bella when she had? Now, to complete the puzzle, she had to help Cara reunite with Dusty.

Hannah hadn't meant to eavesdrop. She'd come to find her earphones, which she knew were in Bella's stable. The yard was quiet after a day full of riding, interviews and filming, dusk settling in the sky above the courtyard. After shutting her chickens in for the night, Hannah headed over to Bella's stable, pausing to admire the neatly swept-up bed and sparkling water buckets all ready for Bella the next morning. It gave her such huge joy to care for the sweet mare.

As she grabbed her earphones, an unwelcome voice drifted over. Ashley. What was he doing in this part of the yard? He was normally in his cottage at this time of the evening, or down in the village in the thatched pub. He was on the phone, and something about his tone made Hannah duck down under the stable door and creep towards the hay net.

"That weird girl who used to be at yours," Ashley was saying. "I swear I saw her here the other day, creeping about with Henry's daughter. Only caught a glimpse, but I'm *sure* it was her."

Hannah felt her blood run cold. She'd thought Ashley had been inside when Cara had come round. She hadn't even considered the likelihood that Ashley would recognise her.

"I don't know. I just have a feeling," Ashley continued. "Too much of a coincidence, surely? Henry's daughter's like a terrier right now, going on and on to Henry about her pony. No, no, he doesn't know that bit," Ashley continued, "and we need to keep it that way. I suggest you get that pony to the next Writley sale. He needs to be gone. Least you'll get something back for him. No one can prove anything after that."

Suddenly Hannah wanted to run to Bella's field, throw her arms round her and never let her go. She remembered what Rollo at Writley Park had told them, about the terrible possibilities that had awaited

Bella. Was that what Ashley meant? For once and for all?

For a few heart-stopping moments Hannah listened to Ashley pace up and down the row of stables. At one point she was sure he peered into Bella's stable and she held her breath, praying he wouldn't look down and see her crouching underneath the hay.

After what felt like an age, she was certain he'd gone. She let herself out and sprinted back to the house. She needed to find out when the next Writley sale was. This was it. This was their chance to be in the same place at the same time as Dusty and bring him home for Bella and for Cara!

Chapter Fourteen

Hannah stared at the laptop screen, feeling her blood run cold. *30 August* was in bold across the schedule she'd downloaded. She looked again, hoping the date would somehow magically change in front of her eyes. But it didn't. The day that had been in the back of her mind for months now, the day that was ringed in red on the yard calendar, the day that would wrap up weeks of intensive filming. The same day as the showjumping championships.

It was also Wolfie's last day with Hannah. Erin was coming with her whole family to pick him up, hopefully after watching Hannah take the much-coveted pony championship title. *Why*, Hannah groaned inwardly, *of all the days, why did they have to clash?*

With a shaking hand, Hannah tapped Cara's name on her phone.

"Hi, Hannah!" Cara picked up quickly, and Hannah could hear some dogs barking in the background. "Hang on a sec. I'm just giving everyone dinner."

Hannah could hear metal bowls clinking, and Cara chatting away to the dogs. She imagined her with the phone on her shoulder, opening tins of food.

"Sorry about that," Cara said. "All done!"

"Cara," Hannah said quietly, "I've found out where Dusty is going. I heard Ashley ... he said something about the next Writley sale. But –" and she paused – "it's the same day as the showjumping championships. The thirtieth of August. I'm so sorry."

"Oh, Hannah, it's OK!" Cara said warmly, but Hannah could hear the faintest trace of disappointment. "You've helped me so much already, getting the paperwork and everything. I'll go to the sale! I'll be fine, I promise. Then I'll come and see you and Bella with Dusty." Her voice faded. "I will."

"I'm so sorry," Hannah repeated. "It's just these championships, my dad, Millie and everything..." she added weakly.

"I'll be OK," Cara said. "I have the passport, and Justine's letter saying he's officially mine." Hannah could imagine Cara's small chin stuck defiantly in the air. "Now you've tracked him down, I'll be able to go and get him." She paused. "I promise," she said firmly. "I'll be OK. Don't worry about me."

The next few days passed by in a blur. Preparation had been upped for the championships, with extra training, extra grooming and extra pressure. The film crew seemed to be around all day, every day, and nowhere in the yard felt safe from the cameras. Millie's video channel and social media accounts were on fire with thousands of messages wishing her luck. Some girls had even booked tickets for the championships solely to cheer her on.

Hannah quietly relished her last few days with Wolfie. She knew she'd cry when she said goodbye, but he had a lovely future ahead of him with Erin. She couldn't stop thinking about Bella's baby and hoped he was well and not frightened. She wished she could communicate with him somehow and tell him it would all be OK soon. In a matter of hours now, Cara would have him back.

He had the sweetest personality, Cara had told her. He was so like Bella. Even though he'd been bottle-fed, he wasn't in the least bit bold or pushy like some bottle-fed foals, and had the cutest way of nudging you gently in the back when he wanted attention. He was cheeky but so kind with it, she'd said. A tear had rolled down Cara's cheek before she'd quickly wiped it away.

Hannah tried to imagine Cara bringing Dusty over to see Bella, and the two ponies reuniting at last, but she couldn't bring herself to picture it fully, not just yet.

Hannah smoothed Wolfie's dark-green travelling rug and gave him a hug. She wondered if he knew he wouldn't be returning the next day. They would be travelling up to the championships tonight for the summer party. In a marquee set up next to the ring the pony showjumping world all got together to dance the night away before the pressure of the next day. Henry would be there for hours chatting to all his old friends, but Hannah planned to sneak away early and read in Wolfie's stable.

Bella watched as they loaded Gem and Wolfie with bright, eager eyes, then gave a whicker as Hannah jumped down from the jockey door.

Millie turned and paused. "Ah," she said. "Look at that. She's really bonded with you, Han. That's special."

Hannah wondered if she could detect the tiniest note of wistfulness in Millie's voice. She knew Millie would find it hard to say goodbye to Gem. Crossing the yard, she gave Bella a big hug, nestling into her silky mane. "I'll see you tomorrow, when I'm back," she whispered. "Send luck for Dusty. You'll see him soon, I hope," she added, hearing the note of doubt in her voice. She wouldn't let herself believe it, not until the little pony was safe.

Henry had asked Vanessa to come and keep an eye on the remaining ponies. Hannah knew Ashley had been sniffy about it, but she also knew he wouldn't want to miss the summer party, so would have to accept it. She hadn't minded going away, knowing Vanessa was overseeing things. Her friend was just as fond of Bella as she was.

It didn't take long to settle Wolfie and Gem into

their temporary stables at the showground, then Hannah and Millie changed into their party outfits. Hannah didn't want to go and she sensed Millie didn't either. Her sister looked really pretty. Her hair was loose down her back and the sequins on her dress shimmered in the evening sun, but her expression was slightly anxious, lost even.

Hannah bit her lip as she noticed girls her age swanning around in trendy outfits, laughing and joking with each other. She looked down at her checked skirt, which she'd thought looked really nice. Now she felt drab and underdressed.

"Hi, Natasha," Millie said brightly, and a girl, arm in arm with another, stopped.

"Oh, hi, Millie," she said.

There was an awkward pause and the girls started to walk away.

"Do you want to catch up later?" Millie said.

Natasha shrugged unenthusiastically. "OK," she said. "If you're about."

"Thanks," Millie said. "It's been ages. I'd love to find out—"

"Remi!" Natasha called to another girl, cutting over Millie. "Sorry, Millie, lovely to see you. I've got to go."

"Sure, yes, OK." Millie stumbled over her words.

But Natasha was off with a flick of shiny brunette mane and a clack of heels. Hannah was sure Natasha's friend glanced back at Millie and said something, and then they laughed. She felt awful for her sister, who was standing awkwardly, plaiting her fingers together.

Hoping to make her feel better, she grabbed them each a Coke, and they sat on the hay bales strewn outside the marquee, watching everyone arrive.

A young woman came over in a white dress. "Hi, Millie? I'm Lizzie. I'm the PA for Rowena Richards, the managing director of Finesse Horseboxes."

Hannah recognised the name of the horsebox company that Millie had mentioned the day Bella had come home. Finesse made the biggest, poshest and most expensive horseboxes on the showground.

Millie smiled at her and stood up, all the awkwardness she'd shown with the other girls melting away. "Hi!" she said brightly. "It's *so* nice to meet you."

"Rowena wondered if you might be free for a chat after your championship class tomorrow? We're just thinking about next year's sponsorship deals and would love to support a young rider."

"Oh wow." Millie looked stunned. "I'd love to. Yes, I'd love to come."

"Great!" Lizzie said brightly, handing over a card.

"That's my number. Good luck in the class; we'll be watching!"

"Oh wow," Millie said again as she sat back down. "That's big."

"It is," Hannah said. She looked at Millie closely as her sister took a sip of her drink. She'd expected Millie to be bubbling over with enthusiasm, to be dancing around as she did at home, but Millie looked quite subdued, as if her mind was on other things. Perhaps it was because of Natasha. But Hannah didn't get a chance to ponder on it because her phone rang. Snatching it up, she made her excuses to Millie and headed off to a quieter area. She had to take the call.

"Cara?"

Hannah gripped the phone. Perhaps Cara had managed to get Dusty back already!

"Hey, what's going on?" Hannah asked. "Are you OK?"

But there was an awful pause at the other end of the phone, and then a woman answered, a voice Hannah didn't recognise. She sounded upset.

"I'm so sorry," she said. "This was the last number Cara dialled. Are you one of her friends?"

"Yes." Hannah felt her stomach drop and her heart begin to race as she clutched the phone to her ear.

"What's happened? Is Cara OK?"

"I don't know," the woman said, her voice breaking. "She's been in an accident."

For a few seconds time stood still.

"An accident?" Hannah whispered, her hands starting to shake. "What do you mean?"

"She was cycling to the shop," the woman said. "I own the kennels she works at. She didn't return for evening feeds, so we went looking and came across the ambulance. The police think she was knocked off her bike." She took a deep breath. "She's such a dear girl. My husband found her phone on the verge once she'd gone in the ambulance, and we thought we'd try her contacts."

"She doesn't really have any family," Hannah said. "Not that I know of. Is she going to be OK?" Her hands were trembling.

"I think so. She was very lucky, they said. She was awake when we got to the hospital, but we weren't allowed in as she was going for surgery on her ankle. She'll be in for a few days, I expect. I'll take her phone to her when I can next visit so you can message each other. I just thought you'd like to know."

"Thank you," Hannah said. She stood for a few minutes after the call ended, just staring at nothing.

Tomorrow was the day of the sale. The last chance to get Dusty back. And Cara was in hospital, and she was here at the show. Suddenly all the glitz and glamour and the glory of the championships felt cheap and worthless compared to saving the pony Cara loved, the pony that wouldn't even be in this dire situation had Bella not been sold off in the first place.

Suddenly Hannah knew exactly what she had to do. She glanced over at Millie who was looking down at the business card, deep in thought. Not even Millie could know, yet, but Hannah was going to get Dusty back.

The first tendrils of light were beginning to creep across the milky night sky as Hannah stretched, sat uncomfortably on an upturned bucket outside Wolfie's stable. She hadn't slept at all in the horsebox living area, finally creeping out a couple of hours ago to sit and wait for dawn. She'd watched some stragglers returning from the marquee after the party, their laughter carrying over to her on the warm night air.

After the call, Hannah had told Millie she had a bit of a headache, but Millie seemed relieved to leave the party as well. Wolfie was asleep at the back of his

A car was going to collect her in five minutes from the main gate. Hurrying over, she jumped as a younger girl almost collided with her. It was Erin.

"Hey," Hannah said, biting her lip. She hadn't wanted to see anyone. "Are you OK?"

"I just wanted to come and see Wolfie," Erin explained. "We're staying at the hotel –" she gestured towards the showring entrance – "and I wanted to wish him luck." Then she seemed to really see Hannah. "Where are you going?"

Hannah glanced down at her trainers and her canvas bag. "I'm going home," she said, as Erin's eyes widened. "Can you do something for me?"

Erin's eyes grew even wider as Hannah explained, but she was nodding and listening intently.

"*Me?*" she said. "I can ride him? In the class?"

"Sure you can." Hannah smiled. "You're more than capable. He's your pony. Enjoy this moment. I left all my show kit for you. The breeches might need a belt, and perhaps you can wear an extra pair of socks with the boots. I left my lucky pin too."

Erin was silent for a few seconds, and then a grin spread across her face. "Actually," she said, "I've got all my riding stuff in the hotel." A blush rose on her cheeks. "Just in case you said I could warm up again."

She looked at Hannah, a flash of doubt on her face. "Do you really think I'll be able to do this?"

Hannah saw a black car pull up outside the main gate. It had to be for her.

"Absolutely," she said, and gave Erin a hug. "Look, there's my taxi. I promise you, you'll be fine. And good luck with Wolfie. He's so special. And I don't mean just because of how big he can jump. Treasure him."

Erin smiled. "I will. Thank you."

Hugging her bag to her chest, Hannah ran to the gates as Erin watched her, before she headed towards the stables with a skip. She looked so excited. Hannah smiled and opened the door of the taxi. "Heartwood, Wolden on the Moor," she said, and the woman driving nodded.

Hannah sank into her seat and watched the showground grow smaller as they drove away.

Chapter Fifteen

Gaby and Jenson were waiting in the yard when the taxi pulled up outside Heartwood's gates. Hannah paid the driver with the cash she'd won at her last show. To her relief Gaby was clutching the envelope with Dusty's papers in it. After the shock had passed, Hannah had called Cara's phone back and asked the lady from the kennels to find the envelope as a matter of urgency. Then she'd called Gaby, who had cycled over to collect it.

There was just one problem. She'd never seen Dusty!

"There's absolutely no record of what he looks like." Hannah riffled through the paperwork. "Height, markings – nothing." The only photo she'd seen of Dusty, the one she'd taken from the caravan and given to Cara, was no help to her. Cara had said he had changed loads since that photo was taken. All Hannah knew was that he was chestnut, and he was greying out. And today would be a big busy sale. What were they going to do?

"Won't he have a name?" Jenson asked.

Hannah shook her head. She was learning fast what things were like. "Bella didn't," she said. "With his legal paperwork here, they won't put him through as Dusty – that would be too risky – and there's no registered name. All I know is that he's chestnut, greying out. I don't know how big or anything!" She slumped against the stable wall. Cara would be going into surgery and still wouldn't have her phone, and it wasn't like she could give Justine a call.

Suddenly a whinny from the other side of the yard, a greeting now she was home, made her look up. In a flash she had the answer. *They* didn't need to know who Dusty was. They needed Bella.

"But how do we get her there?" asked Gaby after Hannah explained. "It's not like we can drive. We can't ask Vanessa – she's already fed the horses and left to see her brother." She bit her lip. "And it's too far to ride Bella to Writley; it'd be dark by the time we got there."

She looked up, and Hannah followed her glance as a familiar figure walked through the yard gates. Freddie. Seeing the trio, he waved and headed over.

"Hey," Freddie said, reaching them. He looked a little subdued. "I'm just picking up my recording stuff. Why aren't you at the championships?"

Hannah thought fast. "My class got postponed until this evening. Something about the ground."

Freddie didn't question her.

Then Hannah frowned. "Why aren't *you* at the championships?" she asked. Normally Freddie followed Millie everywhere, and she knew the championships would be a big content opportunity.

"I was there. It just got a bit … crowded." Freddie shrugged but he looked really dejected. "Logan and Ann-Marie made it clear they could manage without me, and I was slightly in the way. You know me, a bit awkward." He tried to laugh it off, but Hannah could see the hurt in his eyes. She remembered the early days of filming. Freddie's second-hand equipment, making videos in the tack room, laughing until their stomachs hurt. He'd always been so nice, and she felt really sorry for him. Then she had a brainwave. She looked from the Land Rover parked up by the hay barn to Freddie, and back to the Land Rover again.

"Freddie," she said, chewing on a thumbnail, "can you tow a trailer?"

"This is a bit mad!" Freddie said as they reached the end of the winding lanes leading away from Heartwood and headed to the dual carriageway. "Are you sure this is all OK?"

Hannah had told Freddie that Dusty, the pony they were due to collect, didn't travel very well, so needed a companion. *That might even be true*, she thought, a peal of nervous laughter threatening to bubble up inside her.

"Yes," Hannah said, her fingers crossed in her lap. "We just need to go in and get him, and that's it. Don't worry, everyone knows. There was a mix-up with the dates."

"OK." Freddie shrugged. "I'll drop you and while you're there I'll pop to my college – I need to see my tutor before term starts. I'll collect you whenever you're ready; just give me a call."

Hannah didn't want to ask Freddie if he could stay with them, because she knew he'd ring her dad or refuse to let them go if he suspected there was any hint of danger. She had to pretend this was a pre-arranged, totally legitimate thing. "OK," she said, glancing at Gaby, who threw her a worried look. "That's fine."

Freddie drove through the car park and found a space for the truck and trailer, quickly unhitching as Hannah unloaded Bella.

"Let me know when you're ready to go," Freddie said, and then he looked at the auction site, where metal hurdle pens were already full of ponies of all shapes and sizes, tack and harnesses. "*Sure* you're OK?" he asked again.

Hannah smiled brightly. "Course," she said in what she hoped was a breezy tone. "It's all legit. Look." She waved the envelope containing Dusty's paperwork. "We'll be fine."

"OK." Freddie said. "Give me a call if you need me."

Slinging his camera bag over his shoulder, Freddie headed out towards the high street.

Hannah and her friends watched him go.

"Was that a good idea, him leaving?" Jenson said

nervously. "Is it really just a case of going in, getting Dusty and going again?"

"I'm not sure. I've no idea how these things work," Hannah said, clutching the end of Bella's lead rope. "But we're here now. Ready?"

Jenson and Gaby nodded. "Ready."

Bella gave a snort as Hannah led her through the main gates into the auction site, and she seemed to shrink into herself, keeping as close to Hannah as possible.

Hannah gave her a stroke, trying to reassure her. "You're OK," she told the little mare. "I promise you're not being left here."

The group tried to look confident as they circled the pens, hoping to spot a pony who could be Dusty. The auction site was bustling and flooded with noises and smells. There must have been well over a hundred ponies on site, everything from Shetlands to black and white cobs, ponies with dipped backs and big hunter types with gentle eyes. Hannah's heart was racing, and she wanted to cry. She wanted to take them all home. Even though she knew most would go to nice homes, she worried about the few who wouldn't.

But first they had to find Cara's pony.

"What are you doing?"

Suddenly their path was blocked by a tall man. Arms crossed, his bulk filled their path.

Bella snorted and took a step backwards.

"What's that pony doing out?" Everything about the man was powerful and unbending.

Hannah felt the hairs on the back of her neck stand up. She swallowed hard. This felt really dangerous.

"She's my pony; she's not part of the sale," she began. "I'm just trying…" She wondered how to word it. Trying to find a pony they didn't even know?

"I know your type," the man sneered, cutting across her. "Pony-huggers, do-gooders. Think you can rescue a pony. Where are you going to keep it? Your back garden? Come on now." And roughly he grabbed Bella's rope from Hannah's hand. "What pen did this one come from? It needs to go back right now."

Bella rolled her eyes and half reared in alarm, causing the man to lurch and stumble. Righting himself, he swore and raised a fist as if to hit Bella about the face, before Jenson pushed him back.

"Don't you dare," he said, as a trembling Hannah grabbed the rope back.

What had they done, putting Bella into this awful situation? Then, in the distance, there she was. Hannah would recognise the platinum-blonde ponytail anywhere, even though she'd only seen it once. Justine. She was unloading ponies, shoving them forward, slapping rumps hard and forcing them down the ramp. Dusty had to be there somewhere. He had to be.

Jenson looked over and nodded. He had a hand on the man's arm, stalling him. "Hannah," he said urgently. "Run!"

Together Hannah and Gaby ran down the walkway, clutching Bella's mane for support. She seemed desperate to escape the man too.

Reaching Justine's lorry, Hannah desperately scanned the small group of ponies who were now huddled together. All of them looked frightened and bewildered, their coats sticky with sweat, eyes rolling and manes flying. But from among them came a whinny. Bella froze, then lifted her head and whinnied back. It was a feral sound, like nothing Hannah had ever heard before. The call of a mother to her baby. Every hair on the back of Hannah's neck stood up.

"Dusty!"

Bella's head was aloft, her body trembling. It was as if she had tunnel vision. From the group of ponies came another whinny, and Hannah could just make out a chestnut coat with a hint of grey showing through, as Cara had described.

"Here." Hannah thrust Bella's rope at Gaby. "Let me get him."

But a man, seemingly working for Justine, was faster, standing menacingly in her way. He carried four lead ropes and was holding them like a weapon.

"Stop!" Hannah cried. "One of those isn't for sale."

"And what's it to you, little girl?"

Justine. She had been just about to swing the ramp back up but stopped and stalked over to the pen.

Hannah stood her ground. "One of those ponies doesn't belong to you. Remove him from the sale!"

"Get lost," Justine said nastily. "I've no idea what you're talking about. Move along, you little fool."

"No," Hannah said, watching as Bella plunged and reared next to Gaby, who was hanging on grimly. Jenson had been pushed aside by the tall man and was trapped behind him in the surrounding crowd. "I can prove it. Cara? Dusty?" she challenged. "And look, that's Dusty's mother there."

Justine followed her gaze. Not once did her expression change, but suddenly, quick as lightning, she'd opened the hurdle and grabbed Dusty's halter.

"You're mistaken," she said. "Now, for the last time, push off!"

And in one swift movement Justine had shoved Dusty back up on to the waiting lorry. Hannah, still blocked by Justine's helper, finally pushed past him and leapt on to the ramp, but Justine was too fast. Hannah had no choice but to jump down, or risk getting seriously injured as the heavy ramp swung upwards. She could see Dusty's bewildered face, all alone on the big vehicle. Hannah knew that if the lorry left now, she'd lose him forever. She had to stop it.

"This lot giving you trouble, Justine?"

The man who'd blocked them marched up.

"No, no," she said smoothly. "Just a bunch of crazies."

"I'll show you crazy." Hannah felt a bubble of rage build up. Pushing through them, she took the rope back from Gaby, and handed her the precious envelope. She knew the lorry would have to leave from the main entrance to reach the high street.

"Give me a leg up, Gabs," she said, and without even questioning her Gaby placed her hands under Hannah's knee and launched her up on to Bella's back. Hannah gave her little grey pony a stroke. She knew Bella would be terrified.

"Come on, sweetheart," she whispered. "If you do this with me, I promise you'll never have to come to anything like this again. Let's get your baby."

Nudging Bella on with her plimsolled feet, she swung the pony round, almost knocking over the large man who was trying to block her way. She started to canter down the walkway between the pony pens. Glancing back, she could see Justine shouting at the driver to move, and Jenson on the phone as he and Gaby ducked under the man's arm, running as fast as they could. Turning the corner, away from the main site, she saw the lorry heading out next to her, almost parallel.

"Go, Bella, go!"

Urging her on, Hannah clung to her mane. It was like Bella knew what Hannah wanted, as if she knew her foal was leaving and that this was her last chance to save him.

Hannah could see security guards ahead, looking confused and talking into radios. Nearly at the main gates. She had to stop the lorry before it got to the road. She was racing neck and neck with it now, and glanced over at the driver, who looked furious.

"Stop!" she yelled, desperately waving one hand.

"Just stop! You have a stolen pony on board!" But the driver stared straight ahead, changing gear and turning into the gateway at the same moment as Hannah.

"Stop him!" she screamed at the security guards, but quickly realised they were more interested in stopping her, a teenager in shorts and trainers, riding a pony bareback in only a head collar as if she'd just stolen her herself. The lorry was edging through now, and Hannah could taste the dust and fumes in her mouth as she cantered alongside it, desperately trying to claw her way in front. The guards stepped in front of her and lunged for the rope round Bella's neck, causing her to shy away, leaving Hannah scrabbling at her mane as she veered dangerously to the side. If she fell on to concrete, she'd be seriously injured, or worse. With nothing to steady herself, and unable to stop herself slipping, she half fell, half jumped to the ground, feeling the tears coursing down her face as the men closed in, a sea of angry voices and radioed instructions.

In a cloud of gravel dust the lorry came to a juddering halt, and there, like a dream, was the old Land Rover, screeching across the gate entrance, and stopping with a squeal of brakes. Hannah blinked as the driver jumped out and then the passenger. The driver wasn't Freddie. It was the last person Hannah expected to see, because right this minute she should be jumping Gem in one of the biggest, most important classes in her showjumping career.

"Millie?!"

Chapter Sixteen

The driver of the lorry climbed out, red-faced and sweating.

"What's going on?" he demanded, as Justine came striding down from the auction site, her eyes ablaze with anger. Jenson and Gaby were running after her.

"Unload that pony," Gaby said, her dark ponytail swinging as she caught up with the older woman.

"Or we'll call the police," Jenson said, holding his phone up.

"We've got all the proof here." Gaby waved the envelope. "Dusty doesn't belong to you, and he's not yours to sell."

"Is this true?" The lorry driver looked at Justine. "Look, I don't need any trouble…"

"Of course it's not true, for goodness' sake," Justine said crossly. "No one is calling the police. Just carry on with it. *Now*."

"I don't think so." Millie stepped forward, her phone aloft. "I'm filming this," she said with a sweet smile. "You might have heard of me. And if you haven't, let me just say that thousands of people will see this within seconds if I post it."

For a moment they stared at each other, neither backing down. Millie kept smiling, holding the phone in front of her, with not a hint of nerves as Justine glared back. Then Justine scraped her blonde hair back and she rearranged her expression from anger to bland unconcern.

"Must have been a mistake, sorry about that," she said smoothly. "Let's get that chestnut off."

Justine pulled the ramp down, walked up into the lorry, roughly grabbed the pony's forelock and dragged him off.

"There," she said, practically shoving him at

Hannah. "Take him."

Catching her eye, Hannah felt a chill run down her neck. Justine wouldn't forget this.

Dusty, so like his mother with his pretty head and deep dark eyes, scurried over, feet slipping on the concrete, whinnying desperately until he'd reached Bella. The two sniffed noses, clearly talking to each other, each acknowledging that the other was safe. For a few seconds all the noise and chaos of the auction disappeared, and it was just a mare and her baby in their own private world. They were reunited, and for now that was all that mattered.

Freddie had appeared beside Millie and the pair took charge of the situation. Hannah leaned into Bella. She didn't have a lead rope for Dusty, but he wasn't going anywhere; he was almost glued to Bella's side.

The man who had tried to stop them earlier clearly didn't want the police involved, and neither did Justine, but Hannah had a horrible feeling she hadn't heard the last from her. Justine clearly had a lot of influence. Hannah had desperately wanted to save the whole lorryload of ponies, but how? They could help Dusty but were powerless to do anything else. That had to be enough, Hannah thought. For now.

"OK," the tall man said in a gruff tone. "You're free to go." Despite Justine telling him they could take Dusty, he was obviously reluctant to let them leave and did it grudgingly.

Hannah led Bella back towards the main car park and their trailer, ignoring the stares and mutters from sellers. The two ponies loaded easily, their bodies relaxing into each other. Giving them a stroke, Hannah slipped out of the jockey door and turned to face Millie, who had just hitched the trailer back up with Freddie. As Gaby and Jenson piled into the back, the sisters stared at each other.

"I – I don't understand," Hannah said, and Millie gave her a small smile.

"We'll talk later," she said. "For now let's get these two back to Heartwood."

"Where is everyone?"

Hannah looked around the deserted yard, and then back to Bella and Dusty grazing quietly, side by side in the paddock where Hannah's chickens lived.

Millie was leaning against the gate. The two sisters had been watching the ponies for a few minutes. Both had rolled luxuriously in the dust, and Dusty had seemed to visibly sigh with relief as he was let into the field. He sprang through the gate, giving a little joyful kick with his back legs as he headed to the lush grass.

"Ashley and Dad are with Gem and Wolfie," Millie said, and Hannah felt a pang, thinking of the sweet bay pony she'd hugged goodbye only a few hours before. It felt like a lifetime ago.

"You know..." Millie smiled. "That was a great idea to ask Erin to ride."

Hannah turned to her, feeling sick. "How did they do?" she asked nervously.

"They won!" Millie grinned. "They'll be a great team. You should have heard the applause. Erin cried, her mum and dad cried; it was amazing."

Hannah felt a surge of relief. "Oh, I'm so pleased. And what about Gem?"

Millie's smile faded. "I didn't jump her," she said. "And I don't know what's going to happen because of that. But, Han –" she reached for Hannah's hand – "you were right. We did owe Bella. I know where she came from now."

"What? How?"

"The night before we left for the championships, Johno gave me a photo. Look." She reached into the pocket of her riding tights and pulled out a folded picture. "He said he'd been trying to remember when she was here. It's Bella. And me. And look, there's you."

Hannah gazed at the cracked photograph. It showed a younger Bella in the background of what was probably meant to be just a photo of Hannah and Millie. They were hugging, and Hannah was wearing a funny flowerpot hat and red-striped dungarees. But that was definitely Bella. Johno *had* been right. Not that she had ever doubted him.

"You were always so sweet with all the ponies that came in," Millie said. "I remember you hugging and kissing them, even when you were tiny. I bet you did the same with Bella. Even if you can't remember, she can – that's why she felt safe with you. I was going to talk to you when we got home from the championships, but when I found your note, about where you were going today, I jumped in a taxi. Then Freddie rang me – he'd just had this bad feeling – but I'd already arrived in Writley, so I met up with him. I couldn't let you deal with this on your own."

"I had my friends," Hannah said, and then thought about the way Millie had screeched to a halt in the Land Rover, blocking the big horse lorry in. It had been like something out of a film, and she didn't know what would have happened if Millie hadn't shown up when she did. "But I needed my sister. Thank you," she said earnestly. "I'm so glad you were there."

Millie reached over and squeezed her hand, and Hannah squeezed it back.

"Sisters forever," she said quietly, and Millie smiled, a bright genuine smile.

"Sisters forever," she replied. Then she looked up as the chug of an engine approaching grew louder. The big Boland horsebox was pulling into the yard, its sleek exterior shining in the afternoon sunshine. "Now –" she took a deep breath – "let's face the music."

Henry Boland rubbed a hand through his hair, and then placed it on his chin, staring at the girls as they sat opposite him in the office. He looked tired, Hannah thought. The moment he'd jumped down from the lorry, he'd berated them for what they'd done at the market. Hannah wondered how he knew. Perhaps there were people there who knew him and had called him with the news. How much was there about him she *didn't* know? Hannah wondered.

"Do you know how dangerous that was?" he'd shouted. "Stupid, reckless, irresponsible."

Now, in the quiet of his office, it was hard to sum up

his mood. He still seemed angry, but he also seemed resigned.

"We had to get Dusty back, Dad," Hannah said. "We owed him."

Henry looked up sharply. "What do you mean?"

Millie looked at Hannah and pulled Johno's photograph out, laying it flat on the desk in front of their dad. He picked it up and gazed at it.

"That's Bella," Hannah said quietly. "Or Fifty, as she was known when she was sold to a dealer."

Henry was still staring at the photo. "Larkwind Fantasia," he said. "Out of Drifter by Larkwind Candelabra. A perfect mix."

Hannah looked at him, and he passed the photo back with a sigh.

"I knew her, but I couldn't work out why," he explained. "She was here; you were right."

Hannah felt herself slump. She'd known the truth for so long. Why had her dad never listened to her, trusted her, until now?

"What happened?" she asked. "How did she end up like she did?"

Henry shrugged. "Something didn't go right," he said vaguely. "I was still competing, travelling all over, you girls were much younger, so a lot of the work was down to Ashley." He glanced out into the yard towards Ashley's cottage. "We were struggling to get the brand up and running and we couldn't afford to waste stable space on a pony that wouldn't compete. Ashley thought she'd be better in a hacking home, so I let him deal with it."

"But she didn't get to a hacking home," Hannah said. "She got sold to a dealer, the very worst sort, who tried to breed from her over and over." She shook her head, eyes hot and throat growing tight. "Why didn't you check? Why didn't you care enough to find out? What if it had been Mistral or Delilah?" She choked back a sob.

Henry folded his arms. "There's a lot you don't know about this business, Hannah," he said tensely. "It's not all sunshine and rainbows. We are the best, because we sell the best. Only the best."

"So everything that's not the best gets chucked away?"

Henry glared at her. "We have a reputation to uphold. We have bills to pay. Big ones. And every pony here costs a packet in upkeep. Lots depends on our reputation, the horses we sell." He brushed a hand through his hair. "I trusted Ashley to do right by the ponies. Look –" he closed his eyes, as if what he was about to say was particularly painful – "Ashley has been double-crossing me, telling me he'd sold the ponies cheap to good homes. I was happy for him to deal with the ones who didn't make the grade. It meant *I* could concentrate on the big sales. A small loss here and there didn't matter as we more than made up for it with ponies like Wolfie. But he must have been making a profit on the side, either from ponies used to breed or ponies that were then sold on again for a lot of money. He must have been in cahoots with this Justine woman." He swept his hand over his forehead again. "Nothing that I asked him to do was illegal. I just let him get on with things. I didn't question it. I trusted him. He was Johno's boy…" He shook his head. "I let him do it," he repeated in a quieter voice. He looked shattered.

The phone rang, making everyone jump.

Henry answered it, his fingers drumming on the desk. "Right," he said. "I understand. Yes. Thank you."

When he put the phone down he groaned. "That was Horsetalk," he said. "They want to talk to us about breaking the contract." He shook his head. "Running off like that, in the middle of the championships, somewhat upset their filming schedule."

Millie looked at Hannah. "It'll be OK, though?" she said anxiously. "Surely they can take a different angle? Wolfie still won."

Henry leaned back in his chair and sighed. "They didn't sound happy. And Millie," he added, "you can forget the lorry sponsorship. Last I saw they were talking to Erica Headwood." Hannah recognised the name of another popular young showjumper. "Everyone knows you skipped the class. You've got a lot of explaining to do to a lot of people."

He glanced out into the yard again, and Hannah saw Ashley walk across, pausing to look into the paddock where Dusty and Bella were. He looked back over towards the office, his expression unreadable, but Hannah knew he knew.

Henry swung his chair round and stood up, gesturing the girls to leave the office. "I need to talk to him."

Millie looked at Hannah and the girls walked out into the yard, automatically heading over to Bella's paddock as Ashley strode over to their dad, his head held high. He didn't look in the slightest bit worried; he wore the same arrogant sneer as ever. In contrast, Henry looked completely shellshocked.

In the paddock Millie fussed over Dusty while

Hannah stroked Bella, her hands shaking slightly as she ran them over her soft white mane. She tried not to look over at Dad and Ashley, but snippets of their raised voices carried across the yard.

"Is what true?" Ashley's sharp voice rang out. "You told me to sell the ponies. You never worried about where to as long as they were good homes."

"But they weren't good homes!" Henry said. "Not at all!"

"You never looked into it. You were happy not to know. It suited everyone until that pony of Hannah's turned up."

Hannah looked across at the sound of her name.

Henry stood with his arms crossed, shaking his head. "Ashley, I trusted you," he said. "You've done irreparable damage."

Ashley muttered something that Hannah couldn't hear, and suddenly her dad was shouting. "Get out! I want you packed and out of Heartwood. I never want to see your face again."

Ashley shrugged, pulling the same bland expression over his face as Justine had done at the market, and walked away to his cottage.

Hannah looked at Millie and bit back tears. Her dad looked totally broken.

❀ ❀ ❀

The next day at the yard was unbearably tense. Hannah was over the moon she'd been able to save Dusty, but it had come with heavy consequences. She'd had no idea that so much was riding on the final episode of the Horsetalk documentary. She hated to admit it, but she hadn't even thought or worried about it. Padding down into the kitchen early the next morning, she found her mum at the table, nursing a coffee. She was at her laptop, and her eyes were tired and heavily shadowed.

"Are you OK, Mum?"

Hannah sat down next to her, noticing how her mum quickly closed the screen.

Mum smiled, but it didn't reach her eyes. "Yes," she said, but her voice sounded strained. "I'm fine. Just some things to sort out."

"I'm sorry, Mum." Hannah twisted her hands round. "I just wanted to save Dusty. I didn't think about anything else. But it'll be OK. You'll still be paid, won't you?"

"Well –" Lucy ran a hand through her hair, much like Henry had the day before – "that's what we're trying to sort out. And some other things too. There's been some … rumours."

Hannah frowned. "What do you mean?"

"Online and stuff. You know I'm not into that sort of thing," Mum explained. "Anonymous. About the auction, the state Bella was in, Dusty..." Her voice trailed off.

Hannah wanted to close her eyes and disappear. They were her parents, she loved them, but by selling ponies on with an unknown fate, leaving it to Ashley, they'd created a butterfly effect for ponies like Bella to slip further and further into the dark world of neglect. She was so torn. It felt too much to bear.

"Well, whatever happens, we've still got the yard to do." Lucy stood up wearily. "Come on."

"Of course," Hannah said. "Is Ashley really gone?" She couldn't bear to bump into him in the yard.

Her mum took a deep breath. "He's gone," she said. "Apparently a while ago he was offered a job at a polo club, breaking in the youngsters, and last night he agreed to take it, so he's already packed and left." Hannah remembered the expression on her dad's face as he had confronted the groom, and wondered how true that was. "It's for the best."

Hannah winced at the thought of Ashley training other young horses, if he had really been offered another job. But at least he wouldn't be riding their ponies any more.

"What about Johno?"

"We'll look after him," Lucy said. "We always will." She paused, her expression troubled. "Don't ever say anything to Johno about this, will you?"

Hannah knew Johno would be horrified. He would never have sold ponies off like Ashley had – it was his good heart and spotless reputation that had protected Ashley for so long. Her thoughts were all jumbled. Everything was upturned. She wanted to make everything better. But how?

Chapter Seventeen

Hannah helped her mum muck out and feed, revelling in the peace of the early-morning light. She crossed the yard to say good morning to Bella and Dusty and bring them in for the day to the cool of their waiting stables. "You're safe now," she whispered to Dusty. "And Cara will come for you soon, I promise."

Since their success at the auction, Hannah had tried several times to ring Cara but her phone was always off. She couldn't even let her know that Dusty was safe! So as soon as the morning tasks were complete, Hannah had caught a bus to the hospital.

It took several attempts to find Cara's ward, wandering down endless corridors, but finally she reached the right reception desk.

"Hello?"

The woman on the desk looked quite stern but smiled at Hannah.

"I wondered if you could tell me where Cara..." Hannah realised with horror she didn't know Cara's surname. "Where Cara is. With the ankle. I'm her sister," she added unconvincingly, and she knew the woman knew.

"She doesn't have any next of kin listed," the woman said briskly. She wasn't smiling now. "I'm sorry."

Hannah placed her hands on the desk. "OK, I'm her friend," she said desperately. "Can you please pass on a message for me?"

The woman tapped away at her computer, looking over her glasses at Hannah.

"Please just tell her Dusty is safe," Hannah said. "He's at Heartwood with Bella. He's home."

Hannah and Gaby were tidying up the yard. Since

Ashley had left the workload had massively increased and Gaby had agreed to take on some work to keep things going.

Hannah had been waiting anxiously for several days to know whether Cara was OK and had received her message. In the meantime, there had been hushed conversations between her parents, and although Henry had tried to hide it, a couple of letters had arrived with "URGENT" stamped across the top. Hannah felt the weight of what she had done lying heavily upon her.

Gaby leaned on her broom. "It's a bit like old times, isn't it?" she said.

Hannah looked up from her job. "In what way?"

Gaby smiled. "Just us being here together, hanging out."

Hannah nodded and smiled back. "Will you come up here more now?" she asked hopefully.

"I never wanted to stop coming," Gaby replied. "But after Wispa was sold and you were so hurt, it was really hard to be here. But I'm very happy to be back. Plus –" she smiled, throwing a glance around the yard – "it looks like you'll be needing an extra pair of hands around here."

Hannah hugged her friend. It was true. Vanessa

was helping out, but she had other commitments, and Hannah wondered what her mum and dad would do. Between Hannah, Gaby and Millie, they were managing to get all the ponies ridden, and Hannah was spending as much time as possible with Bella and Dusty. With every day that passed, their bond was growing stronger.

"Come on, let's have a break. It's been a busy few hours." Hannah gestured to the bench, and they sat down. They had mucked out fifteen stables and scrubbed endless feed buckets, and Hannah's legs were aching.

Milo, Vanessa's dog, who followed Gaby everywhere, leapt up between them and snuggled down with a sigh. The heat had passed now, and the moors were starting to take on the purple hue of early autumn. Hannah was grateful for the hot-water-bottle warmth of the little dog against her tired limbs and closed her eyes, feeling the weak sun on her face.

"Look." Gaby nudged Hannah's arm.

Hannah opened her eyes and saw a small figure limp through the gates, supported by crutches.

"Cara!" Jumping to her feet, Hannah ran over and gingerly, in case she was still very bruised, gave her friend a hug. Cara clung to her for a few seconds.

Hannah gaped at her. "You didn't walk all this way?"

Cara shook her head. "No. Mrs B dropped me here," she explained. "The kennel owner. I needed to see you. Someone said something in hospital, but I was groggy. Dusty, is he...?" She swallowed hard. "Is he OK?"

Hannah took Cara's arm. "Come with me," she said, and she led Cara through the yard and round by the cherry tree, on towards the paddock where Dusty and Bella stood in contented companionship under the shade of an old oak.

Cara gazed at the sight, and then looked at Hannah, her dark eyes filling with tears. "I – I don't understand?" she said, her voice trembling with emotion. "The championships, the sale. How?"

Hannah smiled. "We owed him," she said.

She didn't tell Cara know about the consequences of her decision to go to the auction, or how dangerous it had been. All Cara needed to know was that her beloved pony was safe and happy.

Cara whistled and Dusty's ears pricked up. He gave a start, and then whinnied, as if he couldn't believe what he was seeing. Then he cantered straight over to where Cara was against the fence and nudged her over and over as if trying to prove she was really there. Cara laughed, and then burst into tears, and Dusty lowered his head and rested it against hers.

Hannah realised she had tears in her eyes, and looking at Gaby, saw that she was also wiping a tear away.

As Cara gently stroked Dusty's mane, Hannah suddenly had an idea.

"Once your ankle heals up, do you know what you'll do?" she asked.

"Well," Cara said, "Mrs B and her husband are selling up, moving to their place in Spain." She looked down. "She said I can stay there while my ankle heals, but after that…" She twirled her fingers into Dusty's soft mane. "I'll be OK. I always am," she said. "Can I pay for Dusty's livery for a few weeks or would you like me to move him now?"

Hannah smiled. "Actually," she said, "I have a better idea…"

"So Cara's starting work here?"

Millie and Hannah were hacking up on the moor. There was a hint of autumn in the air, woodsmoke from a distant bonfire curling through the breeze. Hannah was riding Bella, who was now allowed to go for longer distances. Her ears were pricked and her stride was merry. Millie was riding the lovely German youngster who was jogging slightly at the prospect of the winding open path ahead. Henry had been right; he was a potential world-class star.

Hannah smiled. "Yes. As soon as she's better. And Dusty will stay here with her for good."

She was still surprised that the conversation with her parents had gone so well. With Ashley's departure they'd said that asking Cara to come and work for them was an obvious solution. Hannah suspected that her dad didn't want to draw attention to Ashley's sudden departure by publicly advertising the job.

"That's great," Millie said. "It will be nice to have someone like her around. A friend."

They were silent for a few minutes. Then Hannah asked her sister the question that had been on her mind.

"You've not posted anything in ages," she said. "Is everything OK?"

Millie drew her pony to a halt, gazing out at the moor beneath them. Heartwood was just a speck in the distance now.

"After everything…" She paused. "It just all seemed so … fake. You were right. It was hiding what was going on underneath. I see that now."

Hannah remembered the post Millie had made the day after Ashley had forced Tolly to jump. But she knew what a big deal social media was for Millie. It had been a huge part of her daily life.

"Look," Millie said, taking her phone out and tapping something before handing it to Hannah, "I wanted to show you these."

Hannah looked, scrolling down on the screen, feeling the emotion rise until her eyes filled with tears. Black-and-white photos, head shots of foals, their eyes full of bewilderment, fluffy baby manes a stark contrast with the metal pens they were held in. Steam rising from the back of a group of mares huddled together, the dipped back of an elderly pony walking quietly behind its leader, the proud profile of a bay hunter who was desperately searching for a familiar face. Every photo told a heart-breaking story. Both girls were silent for a few minutes.

"Who took these?" Hannah asked, handing the phone back.

"Freddie," Millie said. "He took them on his way out, after dropping you off, before he rang me. This –" she waved the phone – "this is why I'm not posting. All this is going on *everywhere*, and it turns out we were part of it."

"So what will you do?" Hannah asked, giving Bella a pat.

"I haven't totally figured it out yet," Millie said. "But I'd like your help with something when we get back to the yard. I've got loads of followers who are wondering where I've gone –" she gave a half-smile, the old Millie reappearing – "but I want to do something more than just meaningless showy stuff. I'll carry on what I do, all the social media, but it's going to be different now. I want to do something to make things better." She reached over and put her hand on Hannah's. "You were meant to find Bella. For all of us."

Ann-Marie from Horsetalk was waiting in the yard when the girls returned from their ride, leaning against her car, chatting on her mobile. Ann-Marie didn't look *mad*, Hannah thought, feeling cautious. She looked at her sister, who nodded.

"I called her," Millie said. "I know we broke the contract, but I thought we could take a different angle."

Ann-Marie walked with Millie and Hannah as they dismounted and led the ponies back to their stables.

"I was curious, Millie," Ann-Marie said, patting Millie's pony. "I nearly didn't come, but your message intrigued me. I've spent enough time with you over the summer to know you'd only miss the championships for something pretty huge. So what is it you want to tell me?"

Millie looked at Hannah, and Hannah nodded.

Ann-Marie was silent as she scrolled through Freddie's photos of the auction on Millie's phone. Millie told her about Bella and Dusty, and the race to rescue Dusty. Hannah noticed she didn't mention her parents and Ashley's involvement with it all, and wondered if that would be discussed at all.

"So, you see," Millie said, "I thought perhaps you could cover another angle. Why I wasn't there, what I was doing instead. I'm sure a rescue story would be super popular," she said hopefully, and Ann-Marie nodded.

"I think you're right, it would be," she said. "But I'll need to discuss it with the team. It's not a no – definitely not a no. It's just that I've got lots to sort out after everything was ... well, thrown into disarray."

"Well, that's something we can hope for," Millie said, and gave Ann-Marie her starry smile as they shook hands.

Hannah thought about her dad's exhausted tone when he'd told her about the broken contract. She would never have thought to approach Horsetalk like Millie had. That had taken some guts. She gave her sister a hug.

"I hope it works out."

The beep from Hannah's phone later that evening made her jump. She had just finished cleaning Bella's tack in the kitchen and was on her way out to help bring the ponies in for the night. The number was unknown and Hannah bit her lip before opening the message. She couldn't forget the way Justine had looked at her the day they'd rescued Dusty, as if she were memorising Hannah's face.

Hannah had to read the message several times to make sense of it.

Hey, the message read. *Do you remember my mum? I thought you'd like to know we bought the chestnut mare. Everyone told us it was a bad idea buying from a dealer, but we just fell in love. I know she doesn't like jumping, and it's OK! I don't either. She is so lovely. She has settled in right away. We hack loads, and she'll stay with us for ever. I just wanted to let you know x*

The photo attached showed the woman who had

been heading into Justine's yard when Hannah and her friends had been running away from it. She was holding a lead rope attached to Tolly's bridle and wearing a high-vis tabard. There was a golden Labrador at her feet, and some pretty wooden stables in the background. A girl about Hannah's age in a riding hat was patting the dog, as if they had all just returned from a hack. Tolly looked so content and calm, and so happy.

Hannah felt her heart swell. Everything she'd hoped for Tolly had come true.

But she knew Tolly was one of the few lucky ones. It seemed like an endless uphill task to try to put things right. At that moment sweet Bella crossed the paddock and gently nuzzled her. Hannah smiled and placed her arms round her precious grey mare, hugging her tight. She then fastened her head collar on, ready to lead her into her stable for the evening. As she crossed the yard, she blinked, something on Bella's stable door catching her eye. Moving closer, she felt her heart stop and a lump form in her throat. It was a simple polished wooden sign, the name neatly carved into the oak. *Bella.*

Hannah had no idea who had placed the sign there, but it meant Bella was staying forever. The little mare had come into her life and back to Heartwood for a reason – she knew it. She and Millie were going to be the change. And it was only the beginning of the journey.